喚醒你的英文語感！

Get a Feel for English !

Hospitality English

英語實力與接待能力同步提升，躋身餐旅業 Golden Key 之列！

reservation　check in　handling problems　check out　services

餐旅英文

作 者：David Katz、Victoria Chen

A genuine eagerness to serve is a quality shared by all successful hotel workers. You either have it or you don't, and if you don't, the hospitality industry is clearly not for you. But even if you do have the sincere desire and ability to serve, you must be able to effectively communicate that enthusiasm and expertise. When a guest needs your assistance, earnestly smiling and guessing are poor substitutes for the right words and decisive action.

Written in consultation with managers at the Sheraton Taipei Hotel, Hospitality English provides you with the exact language you need to make warm, authentic connections with the guests you serve. At the critical moment when you are face to face with a guest, a command of this English will allow you to focus entirely on the guest's comfort-and that makes all the difference.

真誠懇切地為客人服務是所有成功的飯店從業人員共有的特質。你也許有此特質,也許沒有。假若沒有的話,餐旅業顯然不適合你。但即使你真的衷心渴望並具備服務的能力,你還必須有辦法將這份熱忱與專業實際展現出來。當客人需要你的協助時,誠摯的笑容與猜測遠不如正確的言語表達及果決的行動來得有用。

《餐旅英文》在編寫時曾諮詢台北喜來登大飯店的經理人,本書提供你所需的精確用語,可幫助你與客人建立起溫馨而真摯的關係。在你跟客人面對面的關鍵時刻,熟稔這些英語表達將使你得以全心全意地讓客人感到舒適,進而使一切為之改觀。

Josef Dolp

Area Managing Director Taiwan, Starwood Hotels & Resorts
General Manager, Sheraton Taipei Hotel
喜達屋集團台灣區總監
台北喜來登大飯店總經理

Preface 作者序

If you thumb through most Hotel English books, you might get the impression that the job of a hotel reservations agent is simply to take reservations. Just pick up the phone and write down the relevant details. Not much to it.

Unsurprisingly, the real world is quite different from the textbook version. In the real world, reservations agents are not telephone operators, but highly skilled sales people. They expertly steer potential customers toward more lucrative rooms and services. They are familiar with the features of every suite, double, and single in their hotel. They know the best way to get the guest from the airport to the lobby. They can calculate agent commissions on the fly and know when a complimentary breakfast voucher will lead to a NT$10,000 sale. Reservations is the hotel's primary profit center, and in the real world, anyone expecting to be hired as a reservations agent must be prepared to do more than check a calendar and copy down credit card numbers.

Our goal with Hospitality English has been to dispense with typical "textbook English" and replace it with the real stuff—the actual words and phrases used every day by leading hospitality professionals in Taiwan.

To this end, we have been greatly aided by the management team at the Sheraton Taipei Hotel. We spoke at length with managers from the hotel's restaurants and guest-facing departments. Through hours of interviews, we gained invaluable insights about what really gets done at a major five-star hotel, and the English that is used to do it. The managers we met with shared stories, training materials, and most importantly, their years of experience on the guest-service front lines. Our sincere thanks to Denhena Chang, Terry Tsao, Melody Liu, Mark Wang, Tracy Koh, and Maria Lin, each of whom contributed immeasurably to the authenticity of the situations and language presented in the book. A special debt of gratitude is owed to Stephanie Pai, who arranged our conversations. We could not have asked for a more capable and supportive guide.

David Katz and Victoria Chen

Taipei, October 2009

若你翻閱大部分的餐旅英文書，可能會得到的印象是飯店訂房人員的工作就是在接受訂房，只要接聽電話，然後把相關的細節寫下來就行了，沒什麼了不起。

不令人意外的是，現實世界跟教科書的內容相去甚遠。在現實世界中，訂房人員並不是接線生，而是技巧高明的銷售人員。他們會巧妙地引導顧客去接受可獲取較高利潤的客房與服務；他們熟悉自家飯店內每間套房、雙人房與單人房的特色；他們知道讓客人從機場來到飯店大廳的最佳方法；他們能即時算出代辦佣金，也知道附贈的早餐券何時能帶來新台幣一萬元的生意。訂房部是飯店的主要利潤中心，而且在現實世界中，任何人想成為訂房人員，他必須準備的可不只是查看日曆及記下信用卡號碼而已。

我們寫作《餐旅英文》的目標是摒棄典型的「教科書英文」，而以符合現實的內容取代──也就是台灣首屈一指的餐旅專業人員每天實際會用到的用語。

為了達到這個目的，我們得到了台北喜來登大飯店管理團隊的大力協助。針對飯店內的餐廳及要面對客人的部門等，我們很詳盡地請教了它們的經理人。經過數小時的訪談，對於五星級大飯店的實際運作情形，以及在此過程中所使用的英文，我們獲得了寶貴的見解。我們所請教的經理人分享了故事、訓練教材，而最重要的，當然就是他們在客服第一線的多年經驗。誠摯地感謝 Denhena Chang、Terry Tsao、Melody Liu、Mark Wang、Tracy Koh 和 Maria Lin，對於本書中所呈現出貼近真實的情境與用語，每一位都貢獻良多。特別要感謝替我們安排訪談的 Stephanie Pai，我們不可能得到比她所給與我們更懇切、更有助益的支持了。

David Katz and Victoria Chen
2009 年 10 月於台北

4

Table of Contents

Chapter Outline

Title Page

以每個主題具代表性的圖像或照片，激發學生之想像力。另一方面引導學生預測整個單元的學習內容及方向，激發學生的學習興趣。

Conversation

每一章皆以 250 字左右、涵蓋該章主要議題的長對話來導入主題內容之學習。藉由在餐旅職場上的實際情境會話，發展學生的字彙與句型應用能力，並培養其透過聽力掌握資訊，以因應未來工作中之基本需求。

Vocabulary

利用形式多元的字彙學習活動（如：分類、填空、配對、翻譯等），培養學生對於專業字彙的理解及應用能力。

Reading / Realia

為閱讀理解練習，題材多為與學習主題相關的實物內容（如：飯店訂房系統操作畫面、餐廳菜單、座位表等）。其目的在於訓練學生靈活運用各章之學習重點、增進英語閱讀理解能力，並熟悉餐旅業工作上常接觸之物件或表單資料。

Sentence Patterns

列舉與該主題內容相關，在實際工作情境中所需具備之重要句型及例句，循序漸進地奠定學生之英語語法及句構觀念，強化表達和溝通能力。

Listening

以大量短對話之克漏字聽寫或選擇等聽力練習，強化學生的聽力，並可作為對主題相關字彙理解程度之檢測。

Advanced Skills

著重在職場溝通上的進階技巧練習，如解決問題、提供建議等，藉以提升學生在工作中面對難題或顧客要求時之溝通及應變能力。

Role Play / Discussion

經由角色扮演或問題討論的方式，檢視學生運用已習得之專業知識和用語的能力，同時可由練習中，提升學生的口語表達能力。

Part I

Hotel

CHAPTER 01

Hotel Reservations

In this chapter ...

■ **Taking Reservations**
Obtaining personal details,
addressing guest requests

■ **Vocabulary**
Hotel rooms, dates, reservation
records

■ **Advanced Skills**
Offering alternatives, upselling,
handling common reservation
problems

Conversation

Listen to the conversation and then take turns practicing it with a partner.

A = Agent   G = Guest

A 訂房組。您好！我是元莉，很高興為您服務！

G Hi. I'm sorry. Do you speak English?

A Yes, of course. My name is Grace. How may I help you?

G I just want to check your availability and get a quote.

A Of course. May I have your date of arrival, please?

G Friday, May 3. I'll need it for four nights.

A Four nights, arriving May 3 and departing on May 7. And what type of room would you like?

G Uh, it's just me, so a single, I guess.

A We have a standard single available for $4,200 per night, and a superior single available for only $4,800. The superior is larger, and comes with a king-size bed and a spacious balcony. May I reserve one of those for you?

G OK, I'll go with the superior.

A Thank you very much, sir. May I have your name, please?

G Jefferson Beha.

A Could you spell your last name please?

G Sure. B-E-H-A.

A B-E-H-A, thank you. May I have your telephone number please, Mr. Beha?

G Sure. It's 0930-976-282.

A Thank you. Would you like to guarantee the reservation with a credit card?

G OK. It's … uh … hold on … The number is 5588 3201 2345 6789.

A Let me repeat that: 5588 3201 2345 6789. And the expiration date is?

G That's right. Uh, the expiration is November 2021.

A Thank you very much, Mr. Beha. I've guaranteed a superior room for you for four nights, arriving on Friday, May 3 and departing on Tuesday, May 7. The room rate will be $4,800 per night.

G That sounds right. Um, I'm a light sleeper, so if possible I'd like to have a quiet room.

A Of course. I'll make sure you get a quiet room overlooking our garden. Your room will be held until 6 p.m. on the day of your arrival. If you need to change your reservation, please contact us before 2 p.m. on the day of arrival or the full room rate will be charged.

G I understand.

A Is there anything else I can help you with, Mr. Beha?

G No, I think that's it.

A We'll look forward to seeing you on May 3, then. Thank you very much.

Hotel Rooms

Look at the pictures, then complete the chart with the common hotel room abbreviations.

Deluxe (dlx)   Single (S)

Double (D)   Suite (ste)

Superior (sup)   Twin (twn)

Room Type	Description
	A standard room for one person
	A standard room with two small beds for two people
	A standard room with one bed large enough for two people
	A large room, often with a queen-or king-size bed
	A large room, often with a queen-or king-size bed and fancy furnishings
	A large room, often with a separate seating area or an additional bedroom

Common Guest Requests

Complete these sentences with the words and phrases in the box.

adjoining rooms	**connecting rooms**	**great view**
airport pickup	**high floor**	**breakfast vouchers**
crib	**late check-out**	**quiet**
rollaway bed (cot)	**early check-in**	**in-room safes**

1. I've never been to Taipei before, so I'd like to use your _____ service.

2. My secretary would probably prefer it if we were placed in _____ rather than _____.

3. I need to rest up for an early meeting, so I'd really prefer a _____ room.

4. Does the discount rate include _____?

5. My son is just ten months old, so we'll need a _____.

6. Our flight doesn't leave until midnight. What's your _____ policy?

7. I'll be traveling with some important documents. Do the suites have _____?

8. I'm trying to impress my girlfriend, and it would really help if I could have a room on a

_____ with a _____ .

9. My wife's brother will stay with us one night, so we'll need a _____ .

10. We'll be arriving before lunch, so I hope you can arrange an _____ for us.

Dates and Duration of Stay

Study the room availability chart below. With a partner, practice making sentences for each of the guests like these:

■ Mr. Beha is arriving on Friday, May 3.

■ Mr. Beha is departing on Tuesday, May 7.

■ Mr. Beha reserved a superior single room for four nights.

■ Mr. Beha will be in room 410 from May 3 to May 7.

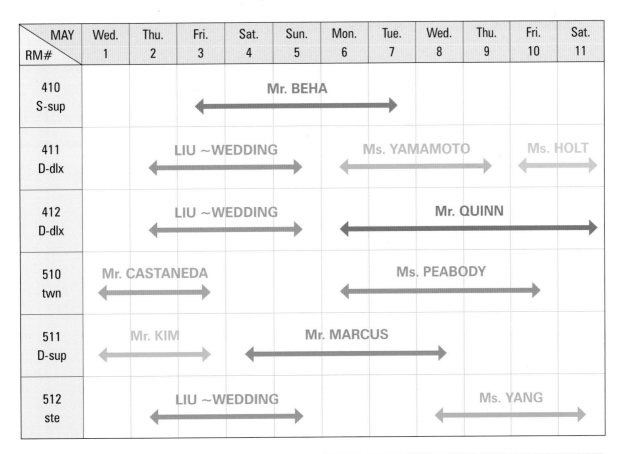

MAY RM#	Wed. 1	Thu. 2	Fri. 3	Sat. 4	Sun. 5	Mon. 6	Tue. 7	Wed. 8	Thu. 9	Fri. 10	Sat. 11
410 S-sup			←——	Mr. BEHA			——→				
411 D-dlx		←—LIU ~WEDDING—→				←——Ms. YAMAMOTO——→				←Ms. HOLT→	
412 D-dlx		←—LIU ~WEDDING—→				←————Mr. QUINN————————————→					
510 twn	←Mr. CASTANEDA→					←————Ms. PEABODY————→					
511 D-sup	←Mr. KIM→			←————Mr. MARCUS————→							
512 ste		←—LIU ~WEDDING—→					←————Ms. YANG————→				

1. Ms. Yamamoto	**4.** Ms. Holt	**7.** Mr. Quinn
2. Mr. Castaneda	**5.** Ms. Peabody	**8.** Mr. Kim
3. Ms. Yang	**6.** The Liu Family	**9.** Mr. Marcus

Completing the Reservation Record

Study the reservation screen that Grace filled out while speaking with Mr. Beha. With your partner, identify the meaning of these abbreviations:

▓ Arr. _____   ▓ Tel. _____

▓ Dep. _____   ▓ Fax _____

▓ ETA _____   ▓ Exp. _____

▓ No. _____   ▓ Conf. _____

▓ VIP _____   ▓ Req. _____

Reservation Record RH98242719

Guest

Mr. / Ms. / Mrs. / Miss _____BEHA, Jefferson_____

Corporate / **Direct** / Group / VIP

Stay

Arr. Date: _May 3_____   Dep. Date: _May 7_____

ETA: _____ Flight No. : _____   No. of Nights: _4_____

No. of Rooms: _1_____   Room Type: _S-sup._____

No. of Persons: _1_____   Rate Quoted: _$4,800_____

Payment

Guaranteed: Yes / No   Credit Card No. _5588 3201 2345 6789_   Exp. _11/2015_

Personal Contact   Business Contact

Tel: _0930-976-282_____   Company Name: _____

Fax: _____   Tel: _____ Fax: _____

Address: _____   Address: _____

Internal

Taken by: _Grace_____   Date: _April 23_____   Conf. Yes / No

Notes: _Req. quiet room. Offered garden view._____

Sentence Patterns

Study and practice these patterns.

Answering a Call

- **Good [time of day]. Reservations. [Name] speaking. How may I help you?**
  Good afternoon. **Reservations.** Grace **speaking.** How may I help you?

- **Thank you for + Ving .... How may I help you?**
  Thank you for calling the Regent Hotel. **How may I help you?**

Determining Details of Stay

- **May I have ...?**
  May I have your arrival date, please?
  May I have your name, please?

- **(And this will be) for ...?**
  And this will be for how many people?
  For how many nights?

- **When will you be Ving ...?**
  When will you be staying with us?
  When will you be departing?

Determining Guest Needs

- **What type of ... would you like?**
  What type of room **would you like?**

- **How many ... would you like to V?**
  How many rooms **would you like to** reserve?
  How many nights **would you like to** stay?

Stating Availability and Tariff

- **We have a ... available on [date] / at [amount].**
  We have a junior suite **available on** June 3.
  We have a deluxe double room **available at** $5,000.

Describing Rooms

- **The [room] has ... / comes with ....**
  The standard twin **has** a coffeemaker and a minibar.
  The executive suite **comes with** a king-size bed and free wireless Internet.

Offering to Make a Reservation

- **May I reserve ...?**
  May I reserve the room for you?

- **Would you like to guarantee ...?**
  Would you like to guarantee the reservation with a credit card?

Asking for Name, Phone Number, and Payment

- **What name ...?**
  What name shall I make the reservation under?

- **Who ...?**
  Who is the reservation for, Sir / Madam?

- **May I have .... , please?**
  May I have your name, **please?**
  May I have your phone number, **please?**
  May I have a credit card number, **please?**

Explaining the Cancellation Policy

- **Please contact us by ....**
  Please contact us by 6 p.m. on the day prior to your arrival to avoid cancellation fees.

Ending the Call

- **Is there anything else ...?**
  Is there anything else I can help you with, Ms. Ito?

- **Thank you for Ving ....**
  Thank you for choosing the Regent Hotel. We look forward to seeing you!

 **Listening**

Listen and complete these conversations.

A = Agent   G = Guest

❶ Determining Details of Stay 🎧 Mp3 03

> **A** Thank you _____ the Beachwood Hotel. Bailey speaking. _____ I help you?
>
> **G** Yes, do you have any _____ available on March _____ ?
>
> **A** Yes, we have a _____ twin available at $3,800 _____ , and a superior _____ available at a special discounted rate of $4,400.

❷ Recommending a Room 🎧 Mp3 04

> **G** What's the difference between the two rooms?
>
> **A** The _____ has two twin beds. The superior has one queen-size bed and a large-screen TV. And it also _____ two complimentary breakfast vouchers.
>
> **G** OK. I'll go with the superior.

❸ Collecting Guest Information 🎧 Mp3 05

> **A** Thank you very much. _____ the reservation for?
>
> **G** My name is Sam Lee. L-E-E.
>
> **A** Thank you, Mr. Lee. _____ your credit card number and expiration date, please?
>
> **G** _____ . And the card expires in _____ .

❹ Confirming Reservation Details 🎧 Mp3 06

> **A** Thank you very much, Mr. Lee. I've _____ a superior _____ room for you for two nights, _____ March 13 and _____ March 15.
>
> **G** Thank you. Um, what's _____ again?
>
> **A** The _____ for the superior is $4,400 _____ . Your credit card won't _____ until you check out.

❺ Explaining the Cancellation Policy 🎧 Mp3 07

> **A** Thank you very much, Mr. Lee. If there are any changes in your travel plans, please _____ 4 p.m. on March 13 to avoid cancellation fees.

⑥ Ending the Call   🎧 Mp3 08

> **A** Is there _____ I can help you with?
>
> **G** No, I think that's it.
>
> **A** OK. Thank you _____ the Beachwood Hotel, Mr. Lee. We look forward to seeing you on March 13.

 # Upselling

The reservations center is about more than matching guests to hotel rooms: It is the hotel's primary profit center. Reservations agents are expected to maximize revenue by encouraging guests to upgrade from standard rooms to superior rooms (and from superior rooms to suites). They are also asked to sell profitable add-ons, such as breakfast vouchers, airport pickup, and special packages. Study the following phrases.

Room Upgrades

▓ For only $800 more, I can upgrade you to a superior room.

▓ I can offer you a suite on the executive floor for an additional $1,200.

Breakfast

▓ Would you like to try our famous breakfast buffet for an additional $200?

▓ We offer a 50% discount to guests who purchase breakfast vouchers in advance.

Airport Pickup

▓ I can arrange a shuttle bus to meet you at the airport if you wish.

▓ The hotel offers limousine service from Taoyuan Airport for $1,800.

Special Packages

▓ The hotel's Garden Spa is offering a 40% discount on facial treatments in January. Would you like me to schedule an appointment for you?

▓ We're offering a special half-day hot springs tour on the 14th. I'd be happy to reserve a space for you.

Practice these conversations with a partner.

1. **Guest:** I just need a standard room.

   Agent: (Upsell: deluxe room) _____

2. **Guest:** Are there any good breakfast places near the hotel?

   Agent: (Upsell: breakfast) _____

3. **Guest:** How much is a taxi from the airport?

   Agent: (Upsell: airport pickup) _____

4. **Guest:** Is there anything special going on that weekend?

   Agent: (Upsell: special package) _____

Handling Special Situations and Problems

How would you handle each of these problems? Write what you would say in the spaces provided and then compare your answers with the responses on page 176.

Availability Problems

A guest requests a single room, but only doubles and suites are available.	A guest requests a room, but the hotel is fully booked.

Payment Problems

A guest wants to guarantee a room, but doesn't have a credit card with him.	A guest feels the room rate is unreasonable, and asks for a discount.

Reservation Changes

A guest wants to postpone his stay by one week and change to a smaller room.

_____

_____

A guest wants to cancel her reservation and make sure she isn't charged.

_____

_____

Telephone Problems

You need to put a guest on hold while you speak with your supervisor.

_____

_____

You cannot understand what the guest is saying.

_____

_____

 # Role Play

Use the vocabulary and phrases you've practiced in this chapter to act out these scenes.

Scene 1

Guest: Reserve a standard twin room on the 15th. Your budget is $2,500.

Agent: Only deluxe ($2,500) single rooms are available on the 15th. The charge for a rollaway bed is $500.

Scene 2

Guest: It's your anniversary, and you want to celebrate in style. You'd like a deluxe double on a high floor with a great view. Your budget is $6,000.

Agent: The only rooms available are a standard twin ($4,000) on the second floor and the Ambassador Suite ($12,000).

 **Discussion**

Do you agree or disagree with the following statements? Why or why not?

1. _____ You never have a second chance at making a good first impression.

2. _____ Even though nobody can see you, it's important to smile while speaking with a guest on the phone.

3. _____ A reservations agent should use a guest's name as often as possible.

4. _____ Reservations is more about sales than customer service.

5. _____ A good reservations agent is more valuable to a hotel than a good front desk clerk.

Discuss the following questions.

1. What's the best way to find a great hotel room at a reasonable rate in Taipei?

2. If you found a good room rate online, would you call the hotel before booking to see if they could beat it?

3. Have you ever asked a reservations agent for a discount? Why or why not?

4. Do you think reservations agents should receive bonuses for successful upselling?

CHAPTER 02

Checking In

In this chapter ...

■ **Checking In**
Welcoming guests, handling luggage, confirming reservation details

■ **Hotel Facilities**
Introducing hotel facilities, describing location, giving directions

■ **Advanced Skills**
Upselling, handling special situations and problems

 **Conversation**

 Mp3 09

Listen to the conversation and then take turns practicing it with a partner.

C = Clerk   G = Guest

C Welcome to the Garden Hotel, sir. How may I help you?

G Hello, I have a reservation. My name is Ashish Parikh.

C Good afternoon, Mr. Parikh. May I have your passport please?

G Sure.

C Yes, I have a standard double reserved for two nights. Is that correct?

G That's right.

C Would you like to upgrade to a superior double for an additional $600 per night? The superior comes with unlimited Internet access and complimentary breakfast vouchers.

G The standard room doesn't come with breakfast?

C Breakfast vouchers for the standard rooms are an additional $250 per day.

G I'll do that, if that's OK.

C Of course. Thank you, Mr. Parikh. That's a standard double for two nights plus breakfast. Would you check and sign the registration card, please?

G Yes, OK. Umm, here you go.

C Thank you. Breakfast is served from 7:00 to 10:00 in Restaurant Fusion, which is next to the guest elevators at the end of this hall. For lunch and dinner, we also have Chinese, Italian, and Japanese restaurants, as well as the lobby coffee shop.

G OK, thanks. And by the way, where is the spa?

C It's in the fitness center. Walk to the end of the shopping arcade and turn left. The fitness center will be on your left.

G Thanks.

C Will you settle your bill by credit card, Mr. Parikh?

G Yes, here you go.

C Thank you. OK, Mr. Parikh, these are your breakfast vouchers, here is your credit card, and here is your key. You're in room 1208. The guest elevators are right around the corner here. I'll have your luggage sent up in just a few minutes. Is there anything else I can do for you?

G No, I think that's it.

C Thank you, Mr. Parikh. Enjoy your stay with us.

▓ **complimentary** [ˌkɑmpləˋmɛntərɪ] *adj.*　免費贈送的

▓ **voucher** [ˋvaʊtʃɚ] *n.*　代幣券；票券

▓ **fitness center**　健身中心

▓ **arcade** [ɑrˋked] *n.*　拱廊

Describing Location

Label the illustrations with the words below.

☐ behind	☐ in front of
☐ between	☐ out / outside
☐ next to / beside	☐ near
☐ far	☐ in / inside
☐ around the corner	☐ across

behind

  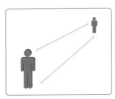
_____ _____

  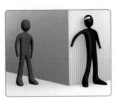
_____ _____ _____

Look at the map on page 22 and practice describing the location of various places around the hotel.

Ex. The business center is across from the meeting rooms.

Ex. The garden isn't far from the parking garage.

_____ _____ _____

Giving Directions

Unscramble the words to form imperative sentences.

Ex. hallway the the to walk of end

Walk to the end of the hallway.

1. up escalator go the _____

2. bakery the at right turn _____

3. arcade the end of the walk shopping to

_____

4. left when you get to shop the turn flower

_____

5. straight lobby go the across

_____

When giving directions, use **imperative sentences** — sentences in which the verb comes first. Despite the serious name, 命令句 are not at all impolite. Actually, they're the clearest way to explain to someone how to get to where they want to go.

Describing Location and Giving Directions

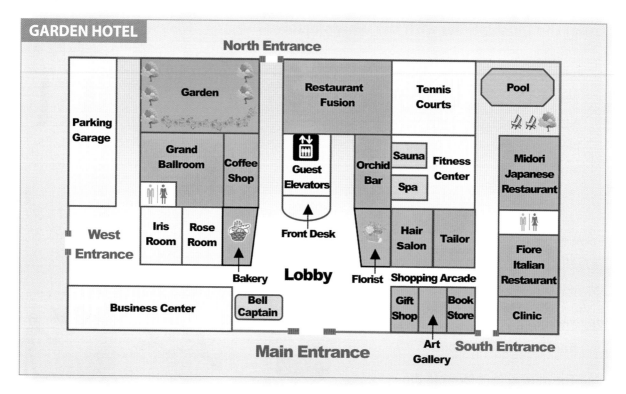

Use the words provided to answer these questions. Then practice asking and answering similar questions with a partner.

Ex. Excuse me, where's the Rose Room? (across from)

   It's across from the Business Center.

1. Is the pool near the parking garage? (no, near)
2. Is the clinic in the fitness center? (no, next to)
3. Do you have a book store? (yes, right next to)
4. Is the hair salon in the shopping arcade? (yes, between)
5. Could you tell me where the sauna is? (sure, inside)

Direct guests from the front desk to these locations.

Ex. Restrooms

   Turn right at the bakery and walk to the end of the hallway. Then, turn right again. The restrooms will be on your right.

1. Elevators
2. Hair Salon
3. West Entrance
4. Midori
5. Gift Shop
6. Clinic
7. Grand Ballroom
8. Tennis Courts
9. Rose Room
10. Parking Garage

Guest Profile

Study the guest profile and answer the questions below.

Guest Profile

Name	STEWART, Andrew Mr.	**First Visit**	2009 01 22
Title	Sales Coordinator	**Total Visits**	11
Organization	Semtech Inc.	**Total Nights**	24
Address	148 Leicester Square	**Usual Rate**	$3,800
	London, U.K. WC2H7LA	**Average Spend**	$4,926
Telephone	+44 (0)20-7724-5122	**Total Revenue**	$118,240
Email	a.stewart@semtech.co.uk		
Passport	U.K. / 817466512		
Payment	Visa 4533 0012 3456 7899		

Comments   CIP, Garden Club Gold
Preferred room: 1608, or other back of building room
On check-in: Greeting by front office manager, fruit basket in room
Service requests: dry cleaning, room service

Record	2009 10 22	Upgraded to Garden Club Gold
	2009 10 21	Complaint: traffic noise (upgraded, moved to back of building)
	2009 09 04	Express dry cleaning
	2009 08 15	Upgraded to Garden Club Silver
	2009 07 01	$5,500 at Business Center (meeting room rental)

1. Why is Mr. Stewart classified as a CIP (commercially important person)?

2. What is the difference between a CIP and a VIP?

3. Why has the hotel kept a record of Mr. Stewart's complaints?

4. Why has the hotel kept a record of Mr. Stewart's address?

5. Not including his room, how much, on average, does Mr. Stewart usually spend at the hotel each day?

Sentence Patterns

Study and practice these patterns.

Greetings

- **Good [time of day]. Welcome to ....**
  Good afternoon. **Welcome to** the Garden Hotel.

- **Hello, [sir / ma'am / name of guest].**
  How are you this [time of day]?
  Hello, Ms. Nakamura. **How are you this** afternoon?

Offering Help with Luggage

- **May I + V ...?**
  May I help you with your bags, sir?
  May I take your luggage for you, ma'am?

- **Let me + V ....**
  Let me help you with those, sir.
  Let me take that for you, ma'am.

Requesting a Guest's Passport or Credit Card

- **I'm sorry, I need to see your [item] for a moment, please.**
  I'm sorry, I need to see your passport **for a moment, please.**

- **May I have your [item], please?**
  May I have your credit card, **please**?

Confirming Reservation Details

- **I have a [room type] reserved for [number of nights]. Is that + Adj?**
  I have a standard double **reserved for** two nights. **Is that** correct?
  I have a deluxe twin **reserved for** one night. **Is that** right?

- **The [room type] is [amount] per night.**
  The standard double **is** $4,800 **per night**.
  The deluxe twin **is** $5,200 **per night**.

Signing the Registration Card

- **Would you + V ...?**
  Would you sign here, please?
  Would you check and sign the registration card, please?

Introducing Hotel Facilities

- **[Meal] is + V ....**
  Breakfast **is** served from 7:00 to 10:00 in the coffee shop.
  Dinner **is** served until 9:00.
  Room service **is** available until midnight.

- **The [facility] is ....**
  The swimming pool **is** located on the roof.
  The fitness center **is** on the second floor.
  The business center **is** open from 7:00 in the morning until 6:00 in the evening.

Presenting Guests with the Key

- **Here / This is ....**
  Here is your key, Ms. Liu.
  This is the key to your room.

- **You're ....**
  You're in 1002.
  You're on the seventh floor, in room 714.

Assisting Guests Immediately after Check-In

- **Let me + V ....**
  Let me take your luggage.
  Let me show you to your room.

- **The (guest) elevator ....**
  The elevator is just around the corner.
  The guest elevators are down the hall.

- **I'll + V + your luggage ....**
  I'll have **your luggage** sent up in just a few minutes.
  I'll make sure **your luggage** is delivered to your room.
  I'll take **your luggage** up in just a moment.

 # Listening

Listen and complete these conversations.

D = Doorman   G = Guest   C = Clerk

❶ Welcoming a Guest 🎧 Mp3 10 ──────────

> **D** Good evening. _____ Garden Hotel.
>
> **G** Thank you.
>
> **D** May I _____ your bags, ma'am?
>
> **G** Oh, thank you very much.

❷ Requesting a Passport and Confirming Reservation Details 🎧 Mp3 11 ──

> **G** Hello, I _____ under Kestler.
>
> **C** Welcome to the Garden Hotel, Ms. Kestler. _____ your passport, please?
>
> **G** Here you go.
>
> **C** OK, Ms. Kestler. I have a superior double _____ nights. _____?
>
> **G** Yes, that's right.

❸ Confirming Room Rate and Signing the Registration Card 🎧 Mp3 12 ──

> **C** The superior double is _____. Would you _____ and
>
> _____ the registration card, please?
>
> **G** Sure. Umm, does that include breakfast?
>
> **C** Yes, it does. I'll give you vouchers for tomorrow and the next day. _____ from
>
> seven to ten in Restaurant Fusion. It's next to the guest elevators at the end of this hall.
>
> **G** Sounds good. Thanks.

❹ Introducing Hotel Facilities ~ Restaurants 🎧 Mp3 13 ──────────

> **G** Are there any restaurants still open?
>
> **C** Yes, Midori, our Japanese restaurant, _____ , and Fiore, our Italian
>
> restaurant, _____.
>
> **G** Do you have any Chinese food?
>
> **C** I'm afraid Chrysanthemum, our Chinese restaurant, is already _____. There
>
> are several Chinese dishes on our _____ though. It's _____.
>
> **G** OK, maybe I'll do that.

25

⑤ Presenting a Guest with the Key 🎧 Mp3 14

C _____ your key, Ms. Kestler. _____ room 1011.

G That's on the tenth floor?

C That's right. Let me _____ the elevator.

G What about my luggage?

C _____ sent up in just a few minutes.

⑥ Introducing Hotel Facilities ~ Describing Location and Giving Directions

🎧 Mp3 15

G Excuse me, is this Chrysanthemum?

C No, this is Midori. Chrysanthemum is _____ . Walk _____ shopping arcade and _____ . Go past the front desk. The elevators _____ .

Upselling

Each of these guests is checking into your hotel. What additional services would you offer to each of them? How would you phrase your offer? (Review the upselling patterns on page 15.)

Name: Brian Pitt
Booking: Superior Single

Name: Jennifer Wheeler
Booking: Standard Single

Name: The Griswald Family
Booking: Standard Twin, 2
Rollaway Beds

Name: Jefferson Kwok and guest
Booking: Standard Double,
Breakfast

Additional Services

room upgrade	executive floor	great view
high floor	connecting rooms	city tour
spa treatment	late check-out	champagne and fruit
massage	flowers in room	restaurant coupons

 # Special Situations and Problems

How would you handle each of these special situations or problems? Use a phrase from the box, or create one of your own.

- Yes, thanks for your patience.
- Of course, sir. I'll have housekeeping take care of that right away.
- We've arranged an upgraded room for you, and will pay for your transportation.
- Let me check to see what we have available.
- I'll get you up to your room as soon as I can, sir.

1. Tired Guest

Guest : I've been on the road since yesterday morning.

Clerk : _____

2. Walk-in

Guest : Hi, do you have any rooms open tonight?

Clerk : _____

3. Long Line of Guests Waiting to Check-in

Guest : You guys sure are busy today.

Clerk : _____

4. Loyalty Card Holder Requests a Free Upgrade

Guest : I think I should be upgraded to a junior suite.

Clerk : _____

5. Early Check-in

Guest : I know it's only noon, but I could really use a shower and a nap.

Clerk : _____

6. Special Requests

Guest : Could I get a crib set up in my room?

Clerk : _____

7. Overbooking

Guest : You're asking me to go to another hotel?

Clerk : _____

 # Role Play

Use the vocabulary and phrases you've practiced in this chapter to act out these scenes.

Scene 1

Guest: You're an elderly Japanese tourist. You can't stand up very long without getting tired. You can't hear very well, and your English isn't that great.

Clerk: Check the guest in and make him or her feel comfortable. If possible, upsell.

Scene 2

Guest: You're a South African business person in Taiwan for an important meeting. You've just arrived at your hotel after traveling for nearly 24 hours. You're exhausted and not in a very good mood.

Clerk: Check the guest in and make him or her feel comfortable. If possible, upsell.

Scene 3

Guest: You're an American parent with two young screaming children, who are probably disturbing other guests in the lobby. Ask about a crib. Ask about the swimming pool. Ask about a city tour. And ask for a free room upgrade.

Clerk: Check the guest in and make him or her feel comfortable. If possible, upsell.

 # Discussion

Do you agree or disagree with the following statements? Why or why not?

1. _____ It's always a good idea to introduce the hotel's facilities before asking the guest for his or her credit card.

2. _____ Any special request made by a guest is an opportunity to upsell.

3. _____ When many guests are waiting to be checked in, it's more important to be fast than to upsell.

4. _____ If a guest's assigned room has to be changed to a very similar room, this should always be referred to as an upgrade, even if the new room is less expensive.

Discuss the following questions.

1. How would you handle a guest who requested an early check-in, but for whom no rooms are available?

2. If two guests arrive at the front desk at the same time, one checking out, and another checking in, who would you serve first and why?

3. If a guest tried to check in using an obviously false name, what would you do?

4. What kind of additional services would you offer to a guest like Mr. Stewart (page 23)? Why?

CHAPTER 03

The Hotel Room

In this chapter ...

■ **The Hotel Room**
Introducing the room, explaining room services and policies

■ **Vocabulary**
Bedroom and bathroom features

■ **Advanced Skills**
Handling problems and complaints

Conversation

Mp3 16

Listen to the conversation and then take turns practicing it with a partner.

B = Bellman   G = Guest

B Here you are, ma'am, room 812. Just slide the key in like this, and when the green light comes on, you can open the door.

G OK, thanks.

B I'll set your luggage over here for now.

G Thank you. Umm, I was told there was a refrigerator in the room.

B Yes, there's a refrigerator and full minibar inside this cabinet, ma'am. And the television and remote control are in that cabinet there, across from the bed.

G Oh, I thought that was the closet.

B The closet is near the door. You'll find extra pillows and blankets, a pants press, and plenty of hangers inside. Oh, and also a luggage rack. Let me get that out for you.

G Thanks. Hmm, it's a bit cold in here.

B Oh, the thermostat is on the wall over here. To adjust the temperature, just turn the knob up or down like this.

G Great, great. By the way, do you guys offer laundry service? I'd like to get this shirt cleaned.

B We sure do. Just fill out this form and housekeeping will take care of everything for you. Shall I ask them to send someone up now?

G No, that's OK. It's not that urgent.

B OK. We also offer daily turndown service. And if there's anything extra you need, you can call the housekeeping office at the number by the phone.

G Thanks. By the way, what time do they come to clean the room in the morning?

B Usually between 9:00 and 11:00. If you'd prefer to sleep in, just hang this Do Not Disturb sign outside the door.

G All right. Sounds good. Thanks for all your help.

B It's my pleasure. I hope you enjoy your stay with us.

▓ refrigerator [rɪˋfrɪdʒəˏretɚ] *n.* 冰箱

▓ minibar [ˋmɪnɪbɑr] *n.* （旅館客房內的）冰箱酒櫃

▓ cabinet [ˋkæbənɪt] *n.* 櫥子

▓ closet [ˋklɑzɪt] *n.* 衣櫥

▓ pillow [ˋpɪlo] *n.* 枕頭

▓ blanket [ˋblæŋkɪt] *n.* 毛毯

▓ pants press 褲子壓摺器

▓ hanger [ˋhæŋɚ] *n.* 衣架

▓ thermostat [ˋθɝməˏstæt] *n.* 調溫器

▓ laundry service 洗衣服務

▓ housekeeping [ˋhausˏkipɪŋ] *n.* 內務；家務

▓ turndown service 鋪床

The Hotel Room

Study these common hotel room items.

FIXTURES

thermostat 調溫器

AC vent 空調通風口

trash can 垃圾桶

black-out curtain 遮光簾

sheer curtain 透明紗簾

SAFETY / SECURITY

safety latch 房門安全閂

peephole 房門窺視孔

sprinkler 灑水器

smoke detector 煙霧偵測器

in-room safe 室內保險箱

ELECTRONICS

telephone 電話

remote control 電視遙控器

television 電視

light switch 照明開關

alarm clock 鬧鐘

DESK AREA

folder 紙夾

tent card 立卡

chair 椅子

desk lamp 桌燈

ethernet jack 乙太網路插孔

BED

headboard 床頭板

box spring （床墊）彈簧層

mattress 床墊

mattress pad 床襯墊

bed skirt 床裙

sheets 床單

blanket 毛毯

duvet 羽絨被

bedspread 床罩

pillow 枕頭

CLOSET / WARDROBE

hanger 衣架

shoe horn 鞋拔

pants press 褲子壓摺器

shoeshine kit 擦鞋包

luggage rack 行李架

laundry bag 洗衣袋

sewing kit 針線包

DRINKS

minibar 冰箱酒櫃

bottled water 瓶裝水

spirits 烈酒

coffee maker 咖啡機

hot water heater 熱水瓶

ice bucket 冰桶

cups and saucers 茶杯和茶碟

creamer / sugar 奶油球／糖

tea bags 茶包

The Hotel Bathroom

Study these common hotel bathroom items.

Bathtub / Bath Linens

showerhead 蓮蓬頭

shower curtain 浴簾

bathrobe 浴袍

bath mat 浴室踏墊

bath towel 浴巾

hand towel 擦手巾

face towel / wash cloth
洗臉毛巾

Counter

tap 水龍頭

washbasin / sink 洗臉盆

drain 排水管

soap dish 肥皂碟

soap dispenser 給皂器

facial tissue 面紙

hair dryer 吹風機

The Wall

retractable clothesline
伸縮式晒衣繩

towel rack 毛巾架

grab bar 扶手桿

fan 風扇；抽風機

shaving (makeup) mirror
刮鬍（化妝）鏡

toilet paper 衛生紙

Amenity Tray

bath cap 浴帽

comb 梳子

shampoo 洗髮乳

conditioner 潤髮乳

facial cleanser 洗面乳

skin lotion 潤膚乳液

floss 牙線

razor 剃刀

toothbrush 牙刷

toothpaste 牙膏

Room Status Terminology

When communicating with colleagues, housekeeping staff use a number of specialized terms and abbreviations to describe the status of a room. See page 177 for a list.

Laundry Service

Study the laundry ticket and answer the questions below.

台北喜來登大飯店
Sheraton Taipei
HOTEL

NAME｜姓名｜お名前	ROOM NO.｜房號｜お部屋番	DATE｜日期｜日付
Peter DeFazio	714	6/24

(V) Regular Service 洗衣服務 一般ランドリーサービス **(V) LAUNDRY** 水洗い
in by 12:00 noon back by 8:00 pm 中午12:00前送洗，下午8:00前送回 昼12時までにご依頼頂けば、午後8時までにご返却が可能です。 水洗
Children 30% off Regular Charge 兒童衣物定價7折 子供服は定価より30%割引きとなります

( ) Express Laundry 快洗服務 快速ランドリーサービス **(V) DRY CLEANING** ドライ
in by 5:00 pm back within 3 hours 下午5:00前送洗，3小時內送回 午後5時までにご依頼頂けば、3時間以内にご返却が可能です。 乾洗
50% surcharge 另加費用5成 は定価より50%割増しとなります

( ) Express Pressing 快速整燙 快速アイロンサービス **(V) PRESSING** アイロン
in by 8:00 pm back within 1 hour 下午8:00前送洗，1小時內送回 夜8時までにご依頼頂けば、1時間以内にご返却が可能です。 整燙
50% surcharge 另加費用5成 は定価より50%割増しとなります

SPECIAL INSTRUCTIONS

( ) Starched｜上漿｜のり付け (V) Shirts Folded｜襯衫摺疊｜シャツを畳んでお渡し ( ) Do Not Crease Trousers｜長褲不燙線｜ズボンのアイロンかけ不要
( ) Heavy Starch｜重漿｜ハードなのり付け (V) Shirts on hanger｜襯衫吊掛｜シャツをハンガーにかけてお渡し ( ) Repair Button｜修補鈕釦｜ボタンの付け直し

CODE NO.	ITEMS			LAUNDRY (NTS)	DRY CLEANING (NTS)	PRESSING (NTS)	GUEST COUNT	HOTEL COUNT	AMOUNT
	Suit(2 Pcs)	西裝(上下)	スーツ（上下）	-	650	(550)	1		
	Coat or Jacket	西上衣	スーツジャケット	350	350	300			
	Trousers	長褲	スーツズボン	350	(350)	300	1		
	Short Pants	短褲	ショートパンツ	250	250	150			
	Blue Jeans	牛仔褲	ジーンズパンツ	350	350	250			
	Shirt/Blouse	襯衫/女衫	シャツ/ブラウス	350	(350)	250	3		
	Sport Pants/Long	運動長褲	ジャージパンツ(長)	200	-	-			
	Sport Pants/Short	運動短褲	ジャージパンツ(短)	150	-	-			
	Sport Shirt	有領運動衫	襟付きポロシャツ	300	300	200			
	T-Shirt	無領運動衫	Tシャツ	300	300	200			
	Skirt	裙子	スカート	350	350	250			
	Skirt, Pleated	摺裙	プリーツスカート	400	420	320			
	Overcoat	長大衣	コート	-	550	450			
	Spring Coat	風衣	スプリングコート	500	550	450			
	Formal Dress	晚禮服	フォーマルドレス	-	600	450			
	Overalls	工裝服	オーバーオール	350	400	250			
	Vest	背心	ベスト	200	200	(150)	1		
	Undershirt	內衣	下着シャツ	85	-	-	4		
	Underpants	內褲	下着パンツ	85	-	-	4		
	Handkerchief	手帕	ハンカチ	50	-	-			
	Socks	襪子	靴下	85	-	-	4		
	Brassiere	胸罩	ブラジャー	85	-	-			
	Hat	帽子	帽子	150	-	-			
	Dress(1-piece)	洋裝	ワンピース	400	450	350			
	Cravat/Necktie	領巾/領帶	クラバット/ネクタイ	-	180	100			
	Scarf/Cape	圍巾/披肩	スカーフ/ケープ	200	200	120			
	Sweater(Wool)	羊毛衣	ウールセーター	-	300	200			
	Pajamas(2-Piece)	睡衣	パジャマ(2ピース)	250	300	200			
	Dressing Gown	晨衣	ガウン	350	400	300			
	Subtotal				10% S.C.		Total		

NOTICE｜注意事項｜ご注意：
* Complete the blanks with your full name, room number and quantity of each article. Unless quantity is specified, our laundry count must be accepted as correct.
* Not responsible for shrinkage or fastness of color, valuables left in or on garments or loss of buttons or ornaments.
* Any claim must be reported with this form within 24 hours. Our liabilities for either loss or damage shall not exceed 10 times the amount of the laundry charge in question.
* All prices are subject to a 10% service charge.
* 請詳細標明姓名、房號、所需洗濯方式（乾、濕、燙）、衣物件數，如未標示，則以本飯店清點件數為準。
* 衣物如有縮水、變色，或貴重物品遺留在衣物內，本飯店概不負責。
* 如對所洗之衣物有任何疑問，請在收到衣物後的二十四小時內，連同清單通知本飯店；若有衣物遺失或損壞之賠償連帶責任，以不超過本洗衣價格之十倍為原則。
* 以上價格需外加一成服務費。
* 請將氏名、客室番号、ご希望の洗濯方法（ドライ・水洗い・アイロン）のほか、数量も正しくお書き下さい。ランドリースタッフが表の数字をもとに、枚数確認を行います。
* 当ランドリーサービスによる衣類の縮みや色あせ、また衣類内に貴重品が残っていた場合も、当ホテルでは責任を負いかねます。ご了承下さい。
* 当ホテルのランドリーサービスに対しご不満があります場合、衣類をお受け取りになられた後24時間以内に、ランドリーリストをご用意の上、当ホテルへご連絡下さい。遺失、損害の連帯責任賠償額は、価格表の10倍を越えないことを原則と致します。
* 上記の料金には10%のサービス料が別途加算されます。

THIS FORM MUST BE COMPLETED AND SIGNED BY THE GUEST｜請詳閱以上注意事項，同意後請簽名
上記の注意事項をよくお読み頂いた後、お客様のサインをお願い致します。

Guest's Signature
貴客簽名
お客様サイン _____ *Peter DeFazio* _____

1. How much will the guest be charged?

2. How much would the guest be charged if he requested express laundry?

3. What special service did the guest request?

4. If a guest needs a dress cleaned, what is the latest time he or she can give it to the hotel?

5. If the laundry service destroyed a hat, what is the hotel's liability?

6. If a guest's wallet gets lost in the wash, who is responsible?

Sentence Patterns

Study and practice these patterns.

Showing a Guest a Room

■ **The N is / are in ....**
  The television **is in** this cabinet.
  The hangers **are in** the closet by the door.

■ **The N is over here / there.**
  The thermostat **is over here.**
  The minibar **is over there** by the refrigerator.

Explaining How Things Work

■ **To V the N, just V the N.**
  To turn on **the** TV, **just** press this button.
  To adjust **the** temperature, **just** turn **the** knob like this.

■ **V the N ....**
  Slide in **the** key to open the door.
  Put **the** Do Not Disturb sign on the door.

Responding to Housekeeping Requests

■ **I'll get you N right away.**
  I'll get you some extra towels **right away.**
  I'll get you a plug adapter **right away.**

Apologizing for Unfulfilled Request

■ **I'm sorry, we don't V ....**
  I'm sorry, we don't allow smoking in the rooms.
  I'm sorry, we don't offer room service after 11 p.m.

Explaining Laundry Service

■ **V the N for N.**
  Please fill out **the** laundry form **for** housekeeping.
  Check **the** boxes **for** the laundry services you want.
  Put **the** laundry bag on the bed **for** housekeeping to collect.
  Call **the** guest service number **for** pick-up.

Reminding a Guest of Hotel Services and Policies

■ **... at [time].**
  Breakfast ends **at** 9:00.
  Checkout is **at** 1 p.m.

■ **Please remember that there is ....**
  Please remember that there is no smoking in the hotel.
  Please remember that there is a charge for the minibar items.

Saying Goodbye

■ **Is there anything else I can V ...?**
  Is there anything else I can help you with?
  Is there anything else I can do for you?

■ **If there's anything we can do for you ....**
  If there's anything we can do for you, let us know.
  If there's anything we can do for you, just pick up the phone and dial zero.

■ **Enjoy your N.**
  Enjoy your stay.
  Enjoy your week with us!

 # Listening

Listen and complete these conversations.

B = Bellman   G = Guest

❶ Showing a Guest Around   Mp3 17

> **B** The clothes hangers _____ .
>
> **G** OK, thanks.
>
> **B** And the luggage rack _____ . Would you like me to put your suitcase on it?

❷ Explaining the Thermostat   Mp3 18

> **G** It's really hot in here. Could you turn up the AC?
>
> **B** Sure. The thermostat is _____ the door. Just _____ the knob _____ if you want to turn up the AC.
>
> **G** Got it. What if I want to turn off the AC?
>
> **B** To _____ the AC, just _____ button here.

❸ Special Requests   Mp3 19

> **G** Could I get some extra blankets for the bed, please?
>
> **B** Certainly. I'll _____ right away.
>
> **G** And a plug adaptor for my laptop, please.
>
> **B** I'm sorry, _____ plug adaptors, but _____ at the hotel gift shop.

❹ Laundry Service   Mp3 20

> **B** _____ I can do for you?
>
> **G** Yes, actually. Where should I put my laundry for the laundry service?
>
> **B** Just _____ your laundry _____ the laundry bag and _____ on the bed for housekeeping.

❺ Hotel Policies   Mp3 21

> **B** Please _____ no smoking anywhere in the hotel.
>
> **G** Yeah, I know. Thank you. What time do we have to check out by?
>
> **B** _____ noon. In the meantime, _____ we can do for you, just _____ !

⑥ Saying Goodbye 🎧 Mp3 22 ────────────────

> **B** _____ I can help you with today?
>
> **G** No, I think we're all set. Thanks for all your help.
>
> **B** It's my pleasure. _____!

Common Hotel Room Problems

Match each of the phrases on the left with the correct ending.

▦ The toilet •	• is flickering.
▦ The air conditioner •	• a pillow.
▦ The remote control •	• isn't flushing.
▦ The ceiling light •	• is out of batteries.
▦ I can't connect •	• isn't working.
▦ The tub •	• any towels.
▦ There aren't •	• is leaking.
▦ We need some •	• smoked in the room.
▦ I'd like •	• more blankets.
▦ The previous guest •	• to the Internet.

How to Handle a Complaint

1. Listen :: Don't interrupt. Allow upset guests to express what is bothering them.

> ▦ *Excuse me, is there something I can help you with?*
>
> ▦ *Could you explain exactly what happened?*

2. Investigate :: Make sure you understand what the guest wants and how he or she wants the situation resolved.

> ▦ *So, the single room is smaller than you expected?*
>
> ▦ *You'd like to upgrade to a larger room?*

3. Empathize :: Show that you take the guest's concerns seriously. Don't argue or make excuses, even if the guest is being unreasonable. You can't "win" a customer service encounter. If appropriate, explain and apologize.

I certainly understand how frustrating that must be.

Room sizes are listed on the website, but you're right, they're not very obvious. I'm very sorry about that.

4. Help :: Solve the problem by offering alternatives, compromises, and suggestions.

Well, our doubles are all full, but I do have an executive suite available. I can offer it to you for the superior double rate of $5,200. Would that work?

I can move you to a double room tomorrow night. Would that be OK?

Handling Special Situations and Complaints

How would you handle each of these special situations or problems? Use a phrase from this chapter, or one of your own.

1. Missing Item

Guest: I'm sorry, I can't find the ethernet jack.

Clerk: _____

2. Need More of an Item

Guest: Hi, I need another set of bath towels.

Clerk: _____

3. Dirty Room

Guest: I don't think the bathroom was cleaned.

Clerk: _____

4. Laundry

Guest: How can I get my laundry done?

Clerk: _____

5. Broken

Guest: The remote control for the TV doesn't work.

Clerk: _____

6. How to Use

Guest: I can't get on the Internet.

Clerk: _____

7. Key in Room

Guest: I think I've locked my key in the room.

Clerk: _____

8. Thermostat

Guest: I can't seem to turn off the air conditioner.

Clerk: _____

 # Role Play

Use the vocabulary and phrases you've practiced in this chapter to act out these scenes.

Scene 1

Guest: You've never stayed in a hotel before, and want to know where everything in your room is located and how each item works.

Bellman: A guest has lots of questions about various room features and items. Try to answer all the questions without going crazy.

Scene 2

Guest: You have many complaints about your room. You are very angry and demand each problem be solved immediately.

Manager: A guest is complaining about his or her room. Try to placate the guest and explain how each problem will be solved.

 # Discussion

Do you agree or disagree with the following statements? Why or why not?

1. _____ The hotel is a "home away from home," so guests have the right to treat their rooms however they want.

2. _____ The hotel's priority is to make guests happy.

3. _____ The best way to handle a complaint is to apologize.

Discuss the following questions.

1. What is the best way to make a guest feel comfortable? Why?

2. How should hotel staff handle rude guests?

3. Is body language important when interacting with guests? If so, what kind of body language should be used? Why?

CHAPTER 04

Hotel Services

Tangy Buffalo Wings
$10.00
With chunky blue cheese dressing and
celery sticks.

Fried Chicken Tenders
$9.00
With French fries and honey-mustard sauce.

Grilled Chicken C
$11.00
Served with
guacamole.

Maryland Cr
$10.00
With red and yello

Hummus
$8.00
With olives and

Soups &
Soup of
$8

Room Service

In this chapter ...

■ **Hotel and Concierge Services**
Determining guest needs, making
recommendations, and following up

■ **Advanced Skills**
Planning itineraries, handling special
requests

■ **Vocabulary**
Words and phrases to offer and
describe services

 # Conversation

Listen to the conversation and then take turns practicing it with a partner.

A = Agent   G = Guest

A Guest Service Center, how may I be of assistance?

G Uh, yeah. This is Stan Miller in 1302. I'm not really familiar with Taipei. Do you guys help guests plan itineraries?

A Yes we do, Mr. Miller. What kind of activities do you have in mind?

G Well, my family and I love to try new food. We were thinking of visiting some good restaurants.

A OK, what kind of food are you looking for? French, Japanese … or would you like to try some local cuisine?

G Something local, I guess.

A Sure. I know a place that serves really great Taiwanese dishes.

G Sounds good. Where is it?

A It's in the Xinyi district, right next to Mitsukoshi — that's a popular department store.

G Oh, all right. Could you make a dinner reservation for us? At about 7:00 tonight?

A Certainly. And shall I arrange for a car to take you there?

G Yes, if possible.

A Of course. I'll have a car waiting for you outside the main entrance at 6:30. Is there anything else I can do for you today, Mr. Miller?

G Yes, I'd like to get a newspaper delivery in the mornings.

A OK. Which newspaper would you like?

G Do you get the *New York Times*?

A We do. I'll arrange that for you right away.

G Thanks. And one more thing — I'd like to take the kids to a museum, too.

A Sure. What kind of museum are you thinking of? An art museum? A science museum?

G An art museum, perhaps. Something more cultural.

A Well, the National Palace Museum is a must-see.

G How do we get there?

A You can take the MRT to Shilin station, and then take a bus. It might be easier to take a taxi, though. Just tell the doorman where you're going and he'll tell the taxi driver.

G All right, we'll do that. Thanks for all your help!

A You're welcome. I hope you have a good time.

▓ itinerary [aɪˋtɪnəˏrɛrɪ] *n.* 旅程；路線   ▓ cuisine [kwɪˋzin] *n.* 烹飪；烹飪法

Hotel Services

Identify the hotel services represented by these icons.

①	②	③	④
⑤	⑥	⑦	⑧
⑨	⑩	⑪	⑫
⑬	⑭	⑮	⑯

_____ ①	Bar
_____	Parking
_____	Hair Salon
_____	Laundry
_____	Childcare
_____	Fitness Center
_____	Swimming Pool
_____	Restaurant
_____	Room Service
_____	Pet Care
_____	Newspaper Delivery
_____	Luggage Storage
_____	Health Clinic
_____	Conference Room
_____	Bicycle Rental
_____	Internet Service

Practice asking and answering questions about hotel services with a partner.

Guest	Guest Service Center
▦ Do you <u>have newspaper delivery</u>?	Yes, we do.
▦ Do you offer <u>luggage storage</u>?	We don't offer ….
▦ Is <u>room service</u> still available?	Yes, it is.
▦ Is the <u>fitness center</u> open?	No, it isn't.
▦ What time does the <u>day spa</u> open?	(Yes,) It opens at ….
▦ What time does the <u>pool</u> close?	(No,) It closes at ….

Concierge Services 1: Questions Guests Ask

Guests often use phrases such as these when asking questions about activities outside the hotel. Translate them into Mandarin.

get something to eat	去吃點東西	go jogging	_____
check out some …	_____	try some local food	_____
do some shopping	_____	meet some locals	_____
get a drink	_____	visit a museum	_____
go for a walk	_____	go dancing	_____
take a tour	_____	get [some place]	_____

If you work in a hotel, you should be prepared to recommend restaurants and tourist spots, and to explain where they are and how guests can get to them. Translate the following phrases, which are often used by both guests and hotel staff.

在這附近	around here	在這個城市	_____
在博物館附近	_____	在捷運站附近	_____
轉個彎	_____	城市的西方	_____
在飯店附近	_____	（從這裡）到那裡	_____
離這裡 10 分鐘	_____	在和平東路	_____

Study the following conversations and circle the activities and underline the location, directions, and transportation options.

Guest: Are there any good places to get a drink around here?

Concierge: There's a great Irish pub on Dunhua North Road. It's just a five-minute cab ride from here.

Guest: Where's Neihu, and what's the best way to get there?

Concierge: It's in the northeastern part of the city. You could take the subway, but from here a taxi would be faster.

Guest: Where can I get a decent hamburger in this town?

Concierge: There are a couple good places near the Taipower Building MRT station. That's just four stops from here on the Green Line.

Guest: Are there any good places near the hotel to try some local food?

Concierge: Of course. There's a great Taiwanese restaurant called Yi Yuan just around the corner. Go straight and then turn right on Ren'ai Road.

Concierge Services 2: Responding to Guest Inquiries

Every concierge has a "black book" full of activity recommendations for every type of guest, from elderly Japanese tourists to young Canadian backpackers. Study the entry from the black book below, and then add descriptions of two locations in your city.

Sightseeing Locations

■ **National Palace Museum**

Description: Premiere collection of Chinese art in the world

Suitable for: All ages, all nationalities. Allow 3 hours.

Transportation: Taxi $340 from hotel; MRT Shilin (transfer to Bus R30); Bus 213, 255, 304, 18, 19

■ _____

Description:

Suitable for:

Transportation:

■ _____

Description:

Suitable for:

Transportation:

Using the vocabulary and phrases on the previous pages and your black book, practice asking and answering questions like the following.

1. What's there to do in this town?
2. Is there a good place to go jogging around here?
3. Where's a good place near the hotel to meet some locals?
4. Are there any museums or art galleries nearby?
5. We want to check out some local handicrafts and maybe do some shopping. Where do you suggest?
6. How can I get to the airport by 7:15 tomorrow morning?

 # Recommending Events

Study the following weekly calendar of upcoming events, and then use it to practice recommending events to the guests below.

Mon. 6	Tue. 7	Wed. 8	Thu. 9	Fri. 10	Sat. 11	Sun. 12
	AmCham Lecture		Baseball		Art and Design Expo	
Taiwan Puppet Show		Basketball			Cloud Gate	Jah Love
	Pottery Talk		Taiwan Jazz Festival			
Beef Noodle Festival				DJ Corndog		E. Chen

Mr. and Mrs. Yamamoto

Interested in Taiwanese culture and food.

Sarah Jensen

Backpacking through Asia. Loves to meet young people and have fun. On a budget.

Kirby Dean

In Taiwan for business. Traveling alone and seems a little homesick.

Live Music

Taiwan Jazz Festival
Renowned local and international artists come together for this world-class four-day jam session.
@National Concert Hall. $800, $1,200, $1,800

DJ Corndog
Hip-Hop Taiwan style
@The Wall 9 p.m. $400

Jah Love
All the way from Puli comes Taiwan's coolest reggae band!
@The Wall 8 p.m. $400

Eric Chen
Solo piano, J.S. Bach
@Taipei Library 2 p.m. Free

Performance

Taiwan Puppet Show（布袋戲）
Shi Yan-wen
@ Puppet Theater Museum 6 p.m. $120

Cloud Gate Dance Theater
"Liao Tianding"
@National Theater 8 p.m. $2,100

Art and Culture

Pottery Talk
Secrets of Ming Dynasty Vases
@National Palace Museum 3 p.m. Free

Beef Noodle Festival
Sample the best noodles in town!
Various locations: see bnf.com.tw

Commerce

Art and Design Expo
See Taiwan's hottest young artists and designers show off their latest creations
@World Trade Center 9 a.m.~7 p.m. $200

AmCham Lecture Series
Prof. P. T. Ma on Taiwan tax policy
@American Chamber of Commerce 1 p.m. $1,900

Sports

Baseball
Brother Elephants vs. La New Bears
@Hsinchuang Stadium 6:30 p.m. $150, $200, $300

Basketball
Taiwan Beer vs. Bank of Taiwan
@Taipei Arena 8 p.m. $200, $500

Kim Soon-ok
Musician and artist looking for inspiration in Taiwan.

Sentence Patterns

Study and practice these patterns.

Offering Assistance

- **Is there anything I can + V ...?**
  Is there anything I can help you with, ma'am?
  Good evening, sir. **Is there anything I can** do for you?

- **How may I be of N?**
  How may I be of assistance?
  How may I be of service?

Determining a Guest's Preferences

- **What kind of ...?**
  What kind of activities do you have in mind?
  What kind of restaurant are you looking for?

- **Are you looking for somewhere Adj. or Adj.?**
  Are you looking for somewhere quiet **or** lively?
  Are you looking for somewhere traditional **or** modern?

- **Would you like to + V ...?**
  Would you like to try some local cuisine?
  Would you like to visit a shopping district?

Making Arrangements

- **Let me see if ....**
  Let me see if any tickets are still available.
  Let me see if I can reserve a table for tonight.

- **Shall I arrange ...?**
  Shall I arrange a car to take you there?
  Shall I arrange a tour of the museum?

Asking for Specifics

- **What kind of ... are you looking for? N? N?**
  What kind of electronics **are you looking for**? Cameras? Computers?
  What kind of Chinese food **are you looking for**? Hakka? Cantonese?

Describing Location

- **It's in ..., right next to ....**
  It's in the Xinyi District, **right next to** Mitsukoshi department store.
  It's in Shilin, **right next to** the Jiantan MRT stop.

- **It's on ....**
  It's on Nanjing East Road.
  It's on the corner of Nanjing and Dunhua.

- **It's a [number]-minute N from [place].**
  It's a five-**minute** drive **from** here.
  It's a ten-**minute** walk **from** the station.

Following Up

- **How was the N?**
  How was the show?
  How was the restaurant?

- **Did you enjoy ...?**
  Did you enjoy the game?
  Did you enjoy your meal?

- **Good! I knew you would + V!**
  Good! I knew you would like it!

- **Oh, I'm sorry to hear that. May I ask why ...?**
  Oh, I'm sorry to hear that. May I ask why you didn't enjoy it?

 **Listening**

Listen and complete these conversations.

C = Clerk   G = Guest

❶ Offering Help 🎧 Mp3 24

> **C** Good afternoon, sir. _____ I can help you with?
>
> **G** Yeah, I have a couple of questions for you.
>
> **C** Sure. How can I _____ today?

❷ Determining a Guest's Preferences 🎧 Mp3 25

> **G** Could you recommend a good restaurant near the hotel?
>
> **C** Certainly. _____ of restaurant are you _____ for?
>
> **G** I'm not sure, actually.
>
> **C** Well, _____ for somewhere _____ or _____ ?
>
> **G** Lively, I think.
>
> **C** There's an excellent hot pot restaurant _____ Songjiang _____ .
>   It's _____ from here.

❸ Making Arrangements 🎧 Mp3 26

> **C** So _____ to see the show?
>
> **G** Yes, it sounds really interesting.
>
> **C** All right. _____ if any tickets are _____ .

❹ Determining a Guest's Needs 🎧 Mp3 27

> **C** Good afternoon. Is there anything _____ , sir?
>
> **G** Yes, I was wondering if there are any electronics stores nearby.
>
> **C** Oh, yes, there are lots. What kind of electronics _____ ? Computers?
>   Cameras? Something else?

❺ Describing Location 🎧 Mp3 28

> **C** How _____ help you?

G Could you tell me where Jasmine Restaurant is, please?

C Sure. It's near _____ Xinyi Road and Yongkang Street. It's about a ten-minute _____ .

6 **Following Up** 🎧 Mp3 29

C _____ restaurant? Did you _____ ?

G It was excellent! Thanks for the recommendation.

C I'm glad to hear that. _____ like it!

Special Service Requests

How would you handle each of these service requests? Use a phrase from the box, or create one of your own.

- Leave it with me. I'll make sure it's sent out right away and charge the postage to your bill.
- I understand, sir. We'll make sure your stay is strictly confidential.
- That's no problem. We contract with a city-certified child-care service.
- Of course, I'll have the bell captain give you a claim ticket.
- Sure. I'll call the garage now and make sure everything will be ready for you.

1. **Luggage Storage**

   Guest: Our flight isn't until midnight. Could we keep our bags here for a while?

   Clerk: _____

2. **Valet Parking**

   Guest: We've got an early morning flight tomorrow. Could you have our car waiting outside at 6:30?

   Clerk: _____

3. **Privacy**

   Guest: We'd prefer not to receive any calls or visitors, if you know what I mean.

   Clerk: _____

4. **Babysitting**

   Guest: My wife and I would like to go out for dinner tonight. Is there someone here who could watch our son?

   Clerk: _____

5. **Packages**

   Guest: I need to send this package to Japan by express mail, but I don't have time to go to the post office.

   Clerk: _____

 # Preparing an Itinerary

Use your own suggestions and the calendar on page 46 to prepare a weekend itinerary for Mrs. Bosch and her husband.

From	jonnah.bosch@gmail.com
To	concierge@jardin.hotel.com.tw
Subject	RE: Itinerary

Dear Concierge,

My husband and I will be staying at the Jardin from May 10 to May 12. As it's our first time in Taipei, we kindly request your assistance in arranging a three-day itinerary for us. We will arrive at Taoyuan International at noon on Friday, May 10 and our return flight departs at 8 p.m. on Sunday, May 12.

We've heard so much about the excellent Chinese cuisine in Taiwan, and we're eager to try all kinds of food—from street stalls to fine dining. In addition to whatever must-see tourist attractions you can recommend, we would love to explore the Taipei art scene. We're especially interested in painting, music, dance, and architecture. Of course we're open to any other suggestions you may have.

I'm looking forward to getting to know a new city. Thank you so much for your help.

Regards,
Jonnah Bosch

April 29, 3:21 PM

Itinerary for Mr. and Mrs. Bosch

	Friday, May 10	Saturday, May 11	Sunday, May 12
08:00-10:00			
10:00-12:00			
12:00-14:00			
14:00-16:00			
16:00-18:00			
18:00-20:00			
20:00-22:00			
22:00-24:00			

 # Role Play

Use the vocabulary and phrases you've practiced in this chapter to act out these scenes.

Scene 1

Guest: You are a food critic and want to try the best restaurants in town. Ask for restaurant recommendations, but be very picky about what you want.

Agent: A guest asks for restaurant recommendations, but is very picky. Try to make suggestions that meet the guest's requirements.

Scene 2

Guest: You are a first-time traveler, and you are very indecisive. Ask the concierge for suggestions about what to do, and ask him or her to do all of the travel planning for you.

Agent: A needy guest asks you to do everything for him or her, but you have limited time because there are more guests waiting to be assisted. Try to help the guest as politely (and quickly) as possible.

Discussion

Do you agree or disagree with the following statements? Why or why not?

1. _____ It is better to recommend a famous restaurant than a restaurant that is not well known.

2. _____ Hotel staff shouldn't recommend places they've never been to.

3. _____ The best way to tell if a hotel is good or not is to see how many services it offers guests.

Discuss the following questions.

1. If you were to make an itinerary for a foreign friend visiting your hometown, how would you organize it? Which places would you recommend? Why?

2. Are there any places in Taiwan that all tourists should visit? Which ones? Why?

3. When traveling, do you prefer to visit places that are famous or places where the locals go? Why?

CHAPTER 05

The Business Center

In this chapter ...

Business Center Services
Offering and explaining services

Vocabulary
Common words and phrases for business center services

Advanced Skills
Addressing problems and special requests

Conversation

Listen to the conversation and then take turns practicing it with a partner.

C = Clerk   G = Guest

C   Good afternoon. Welcome to the business center. What can I do for you?

G   Hi, I'm wondering if I could rent a laptop.

C   Certainly. For how long will you need it?

G   Probably the whole day. How much will that be?

C   Laptop rentals are $500 an hour, or $3,000 a day, not including Internet access.

G   OK, and how much does Internet access cost?

C   It's $300 an hour, or $600 a day.

G   All right, I'll get the laptop, and I'd like Internet access for the whole day.

C   Great. Is there anything else I can help you with?

G   Yes, I'm expecting a fax later tonight, but I'll be away for a meeting. Could you hold it for me?

C   Of course, but I'd also be happy to deliver it to your room.

G   Oh, that'd be better, actually. Thanks.

C   No problem. May I have your name and room number, please?

G   Sure, Sarah Singh, S-I-N-G-H. I'm in room 1306.

C   Got it. Is that all, ma'am?

G   No, I almost forgot! I need to book a meeting room for a presentation tomorrow afternoon. Do you have any rooms open at 2:00?

C   Yes, we do. We have two rooms available tomorrow — the Kenting Room, which seats five, and the Taroko Room, which seats 80.

G   There's probably going to be about 20 or 30 people there, so I guess it'll have to be the Taroko Room.

C   All right. How long would you like to book the room for?

G   Three hours, I guess. From 2:00 to 5:00.

C   OK. I've put your name down for the Taroko Room. I'll have it set up for a presentation for 30. Is that correct?

G   Yes, thank you. Shall I leave my credit card information with you, then?

C   If you prefer. I can also charge everything to your room, if that's more convenient.

G   That would be great. Thanks for everything!

C   You're welcome. Let me get your laptop ready for you, Ms. Singh.

Business Center Services

Use the words in the box to complete the listing of business center services below.

Bilingual Business Cards	Internet Access	Passport Photos
Binding	Interpretation	Photocopying
Booking Tickets	Laptops	Printing
Cell Phones	**Meeting Catering**	Projectors
Conference Room (seats 24)	Meeting Room (seats 8)	Shipping
Confirming Flights	Office Applications	Translation
Fax Services	Packaging	Video Conferencing

Business Center Services

Document Services

- _____
- _____
- _____

Language Services

- Bilingual Business Cards
- _____
- _____

Travel Services

- _____
- _____
- _____

Computer Services

- _____
- _____

Communication Services

- _____
- _____

Mail Services

- _____
- _____

Room Rental and Catering

- Meeting Catering
- _____
- _____

Equipment Rental

- _____
- _____
- _____

Common Business Center Requests

Complete these common requests with the words in the box.

bound	**call**	**check**	**bring**
fax	**make**	**print out**	**printed**
rent	**reserve**	**send**	**translate**

1. I'm expecting an important email from a Mr. Tsai. Could you _____ the attachment when it arrives and _____ it to my room?

2. I'd like to _____ a meeting room for tomorrow afternoon from 2:30 to 4:30. I'll also need to _____ a laptop and a projector.

3. I need to _____ some copies right away. Is there a copier I can use?

4. I'm having trouble reaching my customer. Could you _____ this number and let Mr. Lee know that I'll be late for our meeting this evening?

5. Hi, I need to have a fifty-page report _____ and _____ . Can I have that done here?

6. How much would it cost to _____ these samples to this address by courier?

7. I need to _____ my email. Is there a computer I could use?

8. Do you know anyone who can _____ this contract and then _____ it to this number before the end of the day tomorrow?

Business Center Schedule of Services

Study the following table of services and practice making and responding to the guest inquiries below with a partner.

Business Center Price List

INTERNET

10 minutes or less	$100
30 minutes	$200
1 hour	$300
1 day	$600

FAX

Within Taiwan	$100 / page
International	$250 / page
Received (up to 10 pages)	complimentary
Received (from page 11)	$50 / page

PHOTOCOPYING

Black and white	$5 / page
Color copies	$15 / page
Scanning	$100 / page

PRINTING

Black and white	$50 / page
Color (ink-jet)	$150 / page
Color (laser)	$250 / page

BINDING

Under 100 pages	$400
100-200 pages	$600

MEETING ROOMS

Kenting Room (seats 5)	$1,500 / hour
Yushan Room (seats 15)	$3,000 / hour
Taroko Room (seats 80)	$4,500 / hour
Dongsha Room (seats 150)	$6,000 / hour
Meeting Catering	contact staff for more information

COMPUTER RENTAL

Laptop	$500 / hour
	$3,000 / day
Projector	$300 / hour
Scanner	$200 / hour
Laser printer (toner and paper extra)	
	$350 / hour
Ink-jet printer (ink and paper extra)	
	$450 / hour
Camcorder	$1,000 / day
Digital Camera	$600 / day
Cell Phone	$1,800 / day
	$5,200 / week

INTERPRETATION and TRANSLATION

Professional interpreters and translators are available to assist you. Contact the business center staff for more information.

Prices subject to 10% service charge. All rooms and equipment subject to availability. We welcome reservations, but cancellations less than 24 hours in advance will be charged at the full rate.

EX. 1. Guest: Hi, I need to send a fax to Jakarta. How much is that?

   Clerk: It's $250 per page. How many pages would you like to send?

EX. 2. Guest: Excuse me, do you have computers for rent?

   Clerk: We sure do.

   Guest: How much does it cost?

   Clerk: Laptop rental with wireless Internet is $500 per hour, or $3,000 per day.

3. Guest: Excuse me, [bind a report] _____

   Clerk: _____

4. Guest: Hi, [check my email] _____

   Clerk: _____

5. Guest: Excuse me, [rent a meeting room] _____

   Clerk: _____

6. Guest: Hi, [print a handout] _____

   Clerk: _____

7. Guest: Excuse me, [photocopy a report] _____

   Clerk: _____

8. Guest: Hi, [scan some documents] _____

   Clerk: _____

9. Guest: Excuse me, [translate a brochure] _____

   Clerk: _____

10. Guest: Hi, [rent a cell phone] _____

   Clerk: _____

Sentence Patterns

Study and practice these patterns.

Printing, Photocopying, and Binding

- **If you V, I can print them for you.**
  If you give me your USB drive, I can print them for you.
  If you forward them to me, I can print them for you.

- **How many copies ...?**
  How many copies do you need?
  How many copies shall I make?

- **Would you like the N + p.p.?**
  Would you like the report stapled?
  Would you like the document bound?

Sending and Receiving a Fax

- **It's [price] per / for each page.**
  It's $150 per page.
  It's $250 for the first page, and $100 for each page after that.

- **Would you like me to V the fax ...?**
  Would you like me to forward the fax to your office?
  Would you like me to deliver the fax to your room?

Packaging and Shipping

- **Would you like us to V ...?**
  Would you like us to send the package, sir?
  Would you like us to ship this for you, ma'am?

- **Where would you like (us) to V ...?**
  Where would you like to ship this?
  Where would you like us to send it?

Booking a Meeting Room and Offering Catering

- **We have a room available on / at [time]?**
  We have a room available on Wednesday, the 15th.
  We have a room available at 4:30.

- **We offer N.**
  We offer light catering.
  We offer complimentary water and coffee.

Computer and Equipment Rental

- **We (don't) have [item] available for rent.**
  We have laptops available for rent.
  I'm sorry, we don't have cell phones available for rent.

- **We offer N.**
  We offer complimentary Internet access with all computer rentals.
  We offer Microsoft Word, Excel, and PowerPoint on all of our computers.

- **It's [price] per [time period] to V a N.**
  It's $1,500 per day to rent a laptop.
  It's $250 per hour to use a business center computer.

Translators and Interpreters

- **We (can) provide N.**
  We provide translators.
  We can also provide an interpreter.

- **We will have it back to you in [time period] / by [time].**
  We'll have it back to you in 24 hours.
  We'll have it back to you by 2:30 tomorrow afternoon.

 **Listening**

Listen and complete these conversations.

G = Guest   C = Clerk

❶ Reserving a Meeting Room 🎧 Mp3 31

    G Hi, this is Gerald Dilly in 824. I was wondering if you have any meeting rooms open this Friday.

    C Yes, _____ on Friday, the Kenting Room and the Yushan Room.

    G Which one is smaller?

    C The Kenting Room. It seats five.

    G And how much is it?

    C It's $1,500 _____. For an additional $1,000, _____ light catering. That includes coffee, tea, and snacks.

❷ Renting a Computer 🎧 Mp3 32

    G My laptop just crashed. Do you have a computer I could borrow?

    C You're welcome to use one of the computers here in the business center. It's just _____.

    G No, I need a computer for a presentation.

    C Well, we have a laptop _____. It's _____.

    G OK, does it have PowerPoint?

    C Yes, _____ Microsoft Office on all of our computers.

    G Great. And does that come with Internet access?

    C No, I'm afraid not. There's free wireless in the lobby. Otherwise, Internet access is an additional _____.

❸ Printing 🎧 Mp3 33

    G Hi, I need to print out a few documents.

    C Sure, do you have them on a USB drive?

    G Actually, I've just emailed them to myself as attachments.

    C OK, _____ the business center I can _____. The email address is here on my card.

    G Great, I'll do that now. How much do you charge, by the way?

    C It's $100 _____ and $50 _____.

④ Copying and Binding 🎧 Mp3 34

G Hello, I have a report here that I need copied before tomorrow night.

C OK, _____ do you need?

G Twelve, please.

C OK. _____ stapled or bound?

G If you could just staple them, that would be great. Thanks.

C No problem. I'll _____ 24 hours.

⑤ Receiving a Fax 🎧 Mp3 35

G Excuse me, how much do you charge to send a fax?

C Faxes within Taiwan are $100 _____. International faxes are $250 _____.

G OK. Could you fax this letter to this number for me? And I'll be expecting a reply by fax later today.

C All right. _____ me to _____ the fax _____ when it arrives?

⑥ Mailing a Package 🎧 Mp3 36

G Hi, I don't think I'll have time to get to the post office before my flight.

C Would you like us to _____ for you?

G Yes, please. That would be great.

C No problem. _____ like us to send it?

⑦ Translation Services 🎧 Mp3 37

G Do you offer translation services, by any chance?

C Yes, we do. We can usually have short documents _____ 24 hours.

G Well, I've got a forty-page contract I need translated for a meeting tomorrow morning.

C Well, _____ an interpreter. Perhaps he could help during your meeting?

Computer Problems

How would you handle each of these computer problems? Use a phrase from the box, or create one of your own.

- No, a password isn't required to access the hotel's wireless network.
- The business center sells reasonably priced USB drives.
- Could you check and make sure the wireless switch on your laptop is on?
- I'm not sure. We usually get speeds of ten megabytes per second, even on a wireless connection.
- There's a fee of $400 per day for Internet access. If you'd like, I could connect you right away and have the fee charged to your bill.

1. Charges

Guest: Hi, I'm in room 506. I plugged my computer in, but I still can't get online.

Clerk: _____

2. Internet Access

Guest: There's supposed to be free wireless in the lobby, right? How come I can't get online?

Clerk: _____

3. Password

Guest: Do I need a password to get online?

Clerk: [not required] _____

4. Download Speed

Guest: Do you have any idea why it's taking so long to download this video?

Clerk: _____

5. File Transfer

Guest: I need to move some large files onto my laptop.

Clerk: _____

Printing and Photocopying Special Requests and Problems

Provide translations for the underlined words in the dialog.

G = Guest   C = Clerk

G Excuse me, do you have any idea why my document[1] looks so terrible? The margins[2] are really messed up.

C Let me see … OK, I see the problem. Your document was formatted[3] for 8 ½ x 11 paper, but here we use A4. Let me adjust[4] it for you.

G Oh, that's so much better. Thanks.

C You're welcome. Would you like me to print it out for you?

G Yeah, I need to make a bunch of copies of this report.

C I'd be happy to help you with that.

G How much would that be?

C It's $10 per page for copying, and I could even bind the reports for an additional $50 each.

G Could I just make the copies myself?

C Sure, you can use our copier. It's just on the other side of the printer there. Self-serve[5] copies are $5 per page.

Five minutes later.

G Excuse me, again. I'm getting some kind of error message[6] here. I think there's a paper jam[7].

C Let me have a look … The copier is fine. It's just out of paper. If you'd like, I can set[8] it to make double-sided[9] copies.

G OK, sure. Save a tree. Why not?

C It'll save you some money too. We charge the same for double-sided copies as we do for single-sided[10] copies.

1. document _____

2. margins _____

3. formatted _____

4. adjust _____

5. self-serve _____

6. error message _____

7. paper jam _____

8. set _____

9. double-sided _____

10. single-sided _____

Role Play

Use the vocabulary and phrases you've practiced in this chapter to act out these scenes.

Scene 1

Guest: You have to get a lot of things done in the business center. You're in a big hurry. Ask the clerk for assistance.

Clerk: A guest is in a hurry and comes to you for help. Explain each of the services he or she needs as quickly and clearly as possible.

Scene 2

Guest: You are hosting a meeting in the hotel meeting room, but problems keep occurring.

Clerk: A meeting keeps encountering problems. Try to calm the anxious organizer of the meeting while solving each problem.

Discussion

Do you agree or disagree with the following statements? Why or why not?

1. _____ Hotels should provide free wireless Internet access to guests.

2. _____ The business center is primarily a guest service center, not a profit center for the hotel.

3. _____ Business centers should provide free services to VIP guests.

Discuss the following questions.

1. Is it possible to upsell services at the business center? If so, how? If not, why not?

2. Which business center services, if any, should be complimentary? Why?

3. What are the best ways to encourage guests to use the business center?

CHAPTER 06

The Gift Shop

In this chapter ...

■ Serving Customers
Offering service, responding to inquiries, describing products, payment

■ Vocabulary
Common convenience store and

souvenir items, local handicrafts and specialties

■ Advanced Skills
Handling special situations and problems

Conversation

🎧 Mp3 38

Listen to the conversation and then take turns practicing it with a partner.

Cl = Clerk   Cu = Customer

Cl How are you today? Can I help you find something?

Cu Yeah, I'm looking for something for my wife, actually.

Cl Great. What did you have in mind?

Cu I'm not sure. What is Taiwan famous for?

Cl Well, we have excellent teas. Is your wife a tea drinker?

Cu Yes, she is! Tea sounds perfect. What kinds do you sell?

Cl We sell three different kinds: Oolong, black tea, and green tea.

Cu Which one do you recommend?

Cl It depends. A lot of foreign guests like our green tea. The Oolong is my personal favorite, though. It's stronger and more fragrant.

Cu All right, I'll get the Oolong.

Cl We've got a buy one get one free special on all teas today. Would you like to choose another?

Cu Oh, sure. I'll take the green tea, too.

Cl OK, so that's one bag of Oolong and one bag of green tea.

Cu That's right.

Cl Would you like to pay with cash, credit, or traveler's check?

Cu Cash, please. And could you gift-wrap that?

Cl Of course. Your total comes to $650.

Cu Here you go.

Cl OK, that's $650 out of a $1,000. $350 is your change, and here's your tea.

Cu Great. Thanks for your help.

Cl You're welcome. Have a nice day!

▮ Oolong [ˋulɔŋ] *n.* 烏龍茶

▮ fragrant [ˋfregrənt] *adj.* 芳香的

▮ traveler's check(s) 旅行支票

▮ gift-wrap 將……包成禮品

Common Souvenir Items

Fill in each blank with the English or Chinese word for the souvenir.

keychain

鑰匙圈

shot glass

短袖圓領衫

郵政明信片

打火機

筆

statuette

填充玩具動物

mug

Miscellaneous Goods

In addition to typical souvenirs, hotel gift shops usually sell a variety of other types of goods. Indicate the category that each of the following items belongs to.

■ Over-the-counter medicines (**OTC**)
■ Local specialties and handicrafts (**S&H**)
■ Convenience store items (**CSI**)

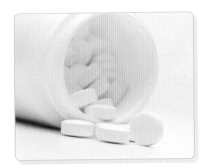

Item: aspirin
Category: _____OTC_____

Item: handkerchiefs
Category: _____

Item: handmade soap
Category: _____

Item: ceramics
Category: _____

Item: tea
Category: _____

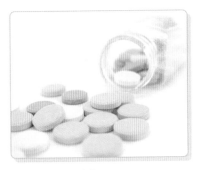

Item: antacid
Category: _____

Item: batteries
Category: _____

Item: bottled water
Category: _____

Item: plug adapter
Category: _____

 # Store Signs

Study the following signs and take turns explaining them to a partner. Use the phrases presented below as a guide.

Save up to 40%

25% Off ~ Discount Taken at the Register

Clearance Sale

Buy Two Get One Free

Free Gift with Any Purchase

Prices as Marked

Spring (Summer / Fall / Winter) Sale

Half Off ~ Today Only

All Sales Final

Patterns

1. Everything (in the store / in this section / on this rack) is ….
2. We're having a ….
3. These items are all ….

Ex: Everything is 25% off today.

Sentence Patterns

Study and practice these patterns.

Offering Assistance

■ **Can I help ...?**
Can I help you?
Can I help you find something?

■ **Are you Ving ...?**
Are you looking for anything in particular?
Are you finding everything OK?

Responding to Guest Inquiries

■ **Yes, the [item] is / are ....**
Yes, the postcards **are** right over here.
Yes, the stuffed animals **are** on your right, on the bottom shelf.

■ **No, I'm sorry ....**
No, I'm sorry, we're out of bookmarks.
No, I'm sorry, we don't sell tea here.

Suggesting Alternatives

■ **You could try ....**
You could try the supermarket across the street.
You could try the 7-ELEVEN on the corner.

Making Recommendations

■ **I think you might V ....**
I think you might like the green tea.
I think you might want to try a smaller size.

Describing Products

■ **This is made of / This was made by ....**
This is made of 100% cotton.
This was made by a local artist.

Offering Compliments

■ **That looks Adj. on you.**
That looks really good **on you**.
That looks a little large **on you**.

■ **You look Adj.!**
You look great! / **You look** amazing!

Describing Discounts

■ **We've got a [special] on [item] ....**
We've got a 30% discount **on** all the shirts on this rack.
We've got a buy one get one free special **on** all clearance items today.

■ **Those are [special offer] today.**
Those are half off **today**.
Those are buy two get one free **today**.

Receiving Payment

■ **Your total comes to [amount].**
Your total comes to $430.

■ **Could you / I ..., please?**
Could you sign here, **please**?
Could I see a picture ID, **please**?

■ **[amount] is your change.**
$70 **is your change**.

Presenting the Receipt

■ **... your receipt ....**
Here's **your receipt**.
Would you like me to put **your receipt** in the bag?

Currency Exchange

■ **You can change currency at ....**
You can change currency at the front desk.
You can change currency at the bank across the street.

Seeing Off a Customer

■ **Is there anything else I can V ...?**
Is there anything else I can help you with?

■ **Thanks for Ving ....**
Thanks for coming. / **Thanks for** dropping by.

■ **Have a Adj. day!**
Have a nice **day**! / **Have a** great **day**!

 **Listening**

Listen and complete these conversations.

Cl = Clerk   Cu = Customer

1 **Helping a Customer**   🎧 Mp3 39

> **Cl** _____ find something?
>
> **Cu** Yes, I'm looking for a souvenir.
>
> **Cl** All right. Are you _____ in particular?

2 **Responding to Inquiries**   🎧 Mp3 40

> **Cu** Do you have any postcards of Taipei 101?
>
> **Cl** No, I'm sorry, _____ those.
>
> **Cu** What about National Palace Museum postcards?
>
> **Cl** Yes, I think _____ some on the top shelf over there.

3 **Describing a Product**   🎧 Mp3 41

> **Cu** Hmm. Do you have any T-shirts?
>
> **Cl** Yes. _____ 100% cotton.
>
> **Cu** Oh, really?
>
> **Cl** Yes, and the artwork on the front _____ a local artist.

4 **Complimenting a Customer**   🎧 Mp3 42

> **Cu** Can I try it on?
>
> **Cl** Sure. The fitting rooms are _____ .
>
> ...
>
> **Cu** So what do you think?
>
> **Cl** Wow, that _____ on you!

5 **Describing a Discount**   🎧 Mp3 43

> **Cu** OK, I'll take the shirt.
>
> **Cl** Great.

Cu Do you have any discounts?

Cl Yes, we've got a _____ special on these shirts today. Would you like to keep looking?

---

6 Payment and Receipt 🎧 Mp3 44 ——————————————————

Cl Your total _____ $499.

Cu All right. Here you go.

Cl Thank you. $1 _____. Would you like _____ in the bag?

---

7 Seeing Off a Customer 🎧 Mp3 45 ——————————————

Cl _____ I can help you with?

Cu No, thanks. I'm all set.

Cl OK. Well, _____. Have _____.

Customer Service

How would you handle each of these customer service situations? Use a phrase from the box, or create one of your own.

A. I'll be with you in just a second.

B. I'm sorry, your card isn't going through.

C. Well, I can hold this for you while you get it, if you'd like.

D. I'm sorry, we only accept Taiwanese currency. You can change currency at the front desk.

E. I'm sorry, we're closed. We open at 10:00 tomorrow morning.

F. Could I see a picture ID, please?

G. We're getting some more in tomorrow. If you'd like, I can have them sent to you then.

H. OK, but you're not going to find anything cheaper than this!

---

1. Try to convince a customer to buy something: ____H____

2. A customer's credit card has been rejected: _____

3. A customer wants to pay with American dollars: _____

4. Verify a customer's credit card is actually his or hers: _____

5. An item a customer wants is out of stock, but will be restocked the next day: _____

6. A customer walks in after closing time: _____

7. A customer needs help but you're assisting another customer: _____

8. A customer left his wallet in his room: _____

 # Returning an Item

Follow the flow chart and familiarize yourself with the phrases for handling returns. Then practice the conversation with a partner.

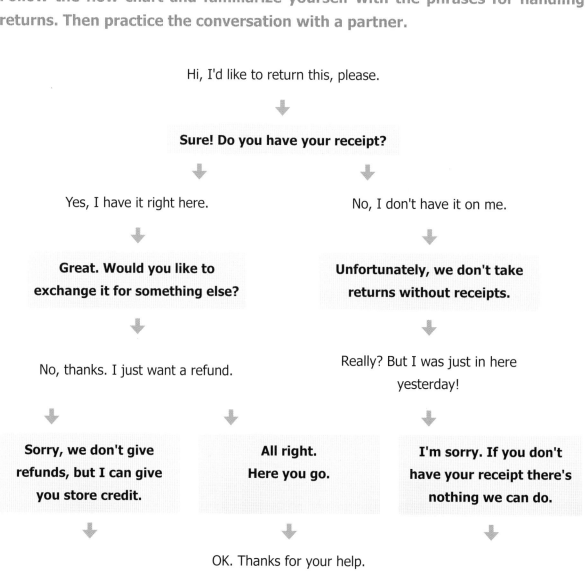

Hi, I'd like to return this, please.

⬇

Sure! Do you have your receipt?

⬇ ⬇

Yes, I have it right here.　　　　No, I don't have it on me.

⬇ ⬇

Great. Would you like to exchange it for something else?　　　　**Unfortunately, we don't take returns without receipts.**

⬇ ⬇

No, thanks. I just want a refund.　　　　Really? But I was just in here yesterday!

⬇ ⬇ ⬇

Sorry, we don't give refunds, but I can give you store credit.　　　　**All right. Here you go.**　　　　**I'm sorry. If you don't have your receipt there's nothing we can do.**

⬇ ⬇ ⬇

OK. Thanks for your help.

Role Play

Use the vocabulary and phrases you've practiced in this chapter to act out these scenes.

Scene 1

Customer: You're looking at something in the hotel gift shop, but you're not sure you want to buy it. Ask for a discount.

Clerk: Try to flatter a customer into buying something. You explain that the item is on sale.

Scene 2

Customer: The item you want is out of stock, so ask the clerk to order it. As you prepare to pay, you realize you left your wallet in your hotel room.

Clerk: Help a customer order an out-of-stock item.

Scene 3

Customer: Try to return an item that you purchased the day before. You don't have your receipt, but you're sure the clerk will remember you.

Clerk: A customer wants to return something without a receipt. Although you recognize him or her, it's store policy not to accept the return.

Discussion

Do you agree or disagree with the following statements? Why or why not?

1. _____ Clerks should always follow store policy, even if the policy is unfair.

2. _____ Clerks should spend more time helping wealthy customers because they usually buy more.

3. _____ It is unfair of clerks to give their family and friends store discounts and benefits.

4. _____ A rude clerk is worse than a rude customer.

5. _____ It is never OK to push a customer to buy something.

CHAPTER 07

Checking Out

In this chapter ...

■ Checking Out
Asking about a guest's stay, explaining charges, offering assistance

■ Vocabulary
Credit cards, traveler's checks, hotel bills

■ Advanced Skills
Handling problems and special situations, guest satisfaction survey

Conversation

🎧 Mp3 46

Listen to the conversation and then take turns practicing it with a partner.

C = Clerk   G = Guest

C Good morning, sir. Are you checking out?

G Yes, that's right.

C May I have your room number, please?

G Yes, it's 604. Here's my key.

C Thank you. Room 604, Mr. Park?

G Yes, that's right.

C All right, Mr. Park, here's your bill. Did you have a pleasant stay?

G Yeah, I had a great time, thanks. The toilet in the bathroom was malfunctioning, though.

C Oh, I'm so sorry. Did someone come to fix it?

G Yes, housekeeping sent a guy up. He fixed it pretty quickly. You guys have excellent service.

C Thank you very much, sir. I'm glad to hear that. If you have a minute, we'd love to get your thoughts about your stay on our guest satisfaction survey.

G Sure, I'll fill out a survey. Excuse me, but what's this $200 for?

C Let me see. Oh, that's for the minibar.

G But I only had water.

C Yes, there's a $100 charge for each bottle of water.

G Oh, Ok … And what about the 5% and 10% charges at the bottom?

C That's a little confusing, I know. The 10% is the hotel service charge, and the 5% is the government tax.

G Oh, all right, then.

C I'm sorry about the confusion. How would you like to settle your bill?

G Do you take Visa?

C Yes, thank you. Please sign here … and here's your receipt. Do you need any help with your transportation?

G Yeah, do you guys have an airport shuttle?

C Yes, it departs from the main entrance every hour on the hour.

G Great. My flight isn't until later, so could I leave my luggage here for now?

C Of course. Let me get you an ID tag for your luggage. You'll need that when you're ready to pick up your bags.

G OK. Thanks for all your help!

C You're welcome, Mr. Park. Hope to see you again soon!

Common Charges and Amounts

Mp3 47

A guest is asking some questions about his bill while checking out. Listen to the conversation, and note how much the guest was charged for each of these services.

spa	$1,000	domestic call	_____
massage (spa)	_____	international call	_____
massage (in-room)	_____	fax	_____
service charge	_____	bar	_____
city hotel tax	_____	minibar	_____
room service	_____	airport transportation	_____
restaurant	_____	airport transportation	_____

Note the different ways of saying dollar amounts.

$850   eight fifty
eight hundred fifty (dollars)
eight hundred and fifty (dollars)

$1,200   one thousand two hundred (dollars)
twelve hundred (dollars)

Credit Cards and Traveler's Checks

Use the words below to complete the conversation. Some words are synonyms, and may be used in more than one place.

accept	call	change	countersign
cover	date	declined	go through
have	pay	provide	raise
run it through	see	swiped	take

C = Clerk   G = Guest

C Would you like to _____ by credit card?

G Yeah, do you _____ Discover card?

C I'm sorry, we only _____ Visa, MasterCard, American Express, and JCB. If your card was _____ when you checked in, we don't need to see it again.

G I don't think it was. Here's a Visa.

C Thank you. Hmm … It didn't _____. Sometimes the magnetic strip gets damaged. Let me try to _____ the machine again.

G Is there a problem?

C I'm sorry, sir. Your card wasn't accepted.

G Is there something wrong with your machine?

C I don't think so. The card was _____. It says that it's over the credit limit. Do you _____ another card?

G No, just the Visa and the Discover card.

C If you like, I can _____ the issuing bank and ask them to _____ the limit.

G Hold on. I think I still have enough traveler's checks to _____ the bill. Traveler's checks are OK, aren't they?

C Yes, of course. I'll just need to _____ your passport, or some other form of identification.

G OK, here you go.

C Thank you, sir. You'll need to _____ and _____ each check.

G OK. Umm, can I get the change in U.S. dollars?

C Well, yes and no. We can only _____ change in Taiwan dollars, but I'd be happy to _____ the Taiwan dollars into U.S. dollars for you. It would be a separate transaction.

G Oh, never mind. I think I might do some shopping at the airport.

 **The Bill**

The Belmont Hotel

No. 46 Chung Hsiao West Road, Sec. 1, Taipei, Taiwan, 100
Tel: 02-2886-6868   http://belmont.taipei.com.tw

Guest Name	CASTANEDA, Raoul Mr.	Folio No.	110315621A
Address	5841 Earle Ave.	Room	1106
	Rosemead, CA 91770 U.S.A.	Room Type	dlxD
Passport / ID	U.S. No. 055702736	No. of Guests	2
Arrive	March 15 Dep. March 17	Rate	4,800

Date	Charges		Amount	Balance
03-15	Room Charges			
-	deluxe double	$4,800/night x 2 nights	9,600	9,600
03-16	service charge	10% ($480 x 2 nights)	960	10,560
	tax	5% ($240 x 2 nights)	480	11,040
03-15	Room Service	21:15	640	11,680
03-15	Laundry	21:40	320	12,000
03-15	2nd Street Restaurant	13:28	580	12,580
03-16	Business Center	09:07	180	12,760
03-16	2nd Street Restaurant	20:44	1,320	14,080
03-17	Minibar	11:19	160	14,240
03-17	Airport Limousine	11:21	1,800	16,040
	(less deposit / amount paid)			- 0.00
	Deposit MasterCard XXXX-XXXX-XXXX-X824			
			Amount Due:	$16,040

Thank you for choosing the Belmont Hotel. We look forward to serving you again.

If payment is by credit card, the hotel is authorized to bill my account for all goods and services rendered, including applicable taxes, a minimum ten percent service charge, and costs resulting from missing or damaged items. I agree to be personally liable for all payments charged to my account.

Guest Signature   *R. Castaneda*   Date   3/17

With a partner, practice asking and answering questions like these:

- What's this charge for?
- What is this 5% charge, here?
- I don't remember making so many international calls.
- I think there's a mistake here.
- Are you sure about this amount?
- One hundred and sixty dollars for a small bottle of water? Is that right?

Sentence Patterns

Study and practice these patterns.

Confirming Check-Out

■ **Good [time of day], sir / ma'am. Are you ...?**
Good morning, **sir. Are you** checking out?
Good afternoon, **ma'am. Are you** ready to check out?

■ **May I have your ...?**
May I have your room number, please?
May I have your key, please?

Inquiring About a Guest's Stay

■ **How was + N?**
How was your stay?
How was everything?

■ **Did you + V ...?**
Did you have a good stay?
Did you enjoy your stay?

■ **I'm ... to hear that.**
I'm glad **to hear that**. Thank you very much.
I'm sorry **to hear that**. May I ask why?

Preparing the Bill, Asking for Payment

■ **Just a moment, [name]. I'm V your bill now.**
Just a moment, Ms. Costa. **I'm** preparing **your bill now**.
Just a moment, Mr. Atkinson. **I'm** printing **your bill now**.

■ **How would you like to V your bill?**
How would you like to settle **your bill**?
How would you like to pay **your bill**?

■ **Please V the bill and + V.**
Please check **the bill and** sign here.
Please review **the bill and** then date and countersign each check.

Explaining Charges

■ **That's the + N.**
That's the service charge.
That's the government tax.

■ **This / That (amount) is for + N.**
This $1,350 **is for** room service.
That's for the spa.

■ **This was / will be Ved to your ....**
This was billed **to your** room.
This will not be charged **to your** credit card.

Offering Assistance

■ **Do you need help with your ...?**
Do you need help with your luggage?
Do you need help with your transportation?

■ **We offer complimentary ....**
We offer complimentary luggage storage.
We offer complimentary shuttle service to the airport.

Seeing Off a Guest

■ **Thank you for choosing [hotel name].**
Thank you for choosing the Taipei Sheraton.

■ **Have a Adj. trip.**
Have a safe **trip**.
Have a good **trip**.

■ **We hope ....**
We hope you enjoyed your stay with us.
We hope to see you again soon.

 # Listening

Listen and complete these conversations.

C = Clerk   G = Guest

❶ Confirming Check-Out 🎧 Mp3 48

> **C** _____, ma'am. Are you _____?
>
> **G** Yes, I am.
>
> **C** All right. May I have your _____, please?

❷ Inquiring About a Guest's Stay 🎧 Mp3 49

> **C** How was _____? Did you have a _____?
>
> **G** It could've been better, to be honest.
>
> **C** I'm so _____! May I ask why?
>
> **G** Well, I couldn't sleep very well because of the noise going on outside.
>
> **C** Oh, I'll let our manager know about that right away.

❸ Presenting the Bill 🎧 Mp3 50

> **C** Please wait _____. I'm _____ your bill right now.
>
> **G** Sure. Take your time.
>
> **C** OK, here you go. How would you like to _____?
>
> **G** Do you take traveler's checks?
>
> **C** Yes, we do. Please _____ the bill, then _____ and _____ each check.

❹ Explaining the Bill 🎧 Mp3 51

> **G** What's this for?
>
> **C** That's for the _____.
>
> **G** But I never even opened the minibar.
>
> **C** Oh, I'm sorry. I'll remove that from the bill and make sure it _____ credit card.
>
> **G** Thanks. And what about this?
>
> **C** That's the _____.

5 Offering Assistance 🎧 Mp3 52

C _____ with your transportation to the airport?

G Yeah, is there a shuttle I can take?

C Yes, _____ shuttle service to the airport. Let me check the schedule ... OK, the next one leaves at 2:00.

G Oh, that's great. Thank you. Can I leave my suitcase here while I get some lunch?

C Of course. _____ luggage storage too.

6 Seeing Off a Guest 🎧 Mp3 53

C Is there anything else I can help you with?

G Nope, I think that's it. Thanks.

C It's our pleasure. Thank you for _____ the Taipei Sheraton. Have _____!

Special Situations and Problems

How would you handle each of these special situations or problems? Use a phrase from the box, or create one of your own.

- Yes, you'll be credited with one mile for every five dollars you spend.
- I'm sorry. We're not able to offer cash advances. There's a bank around the corner.
- Yes, there is, sir. I'd be happy to make a booking for you.
- Gold Club members can check out any time before four o'clock.
- Well, there may be a foreign currency surcharge, but that's set by the issuing bank.
- Yes, the duty manager has agreed to refund the additional charge. I'll need to see your credit card again so I can do a chargeback.
- Well, let me confirm that. I'll print out a copy of our phone records.

1. **Late Checkout**

   Guest: I've got a Gold Club card. Does that allow me to check out a little later?

   Clerk: _____

2. **Frequent Flyer Program**

   Guest: I think I'm supposed to be getting airline miles with my stay here.

   Clerk: _____

83

3. Onward Booking

Guest: There's not a Sheraton in Sapporo, is there?

Clerk: _____

4. Extra Charges

Guest: I don't remember making that many calls from my room.

Clerk: _____

5. Foreign Credit Card

Guest: Is it going to be really expensive for me to use my Canadian credit card?

Clerk: _____

6. Cash Advance

Guest: Could I use my card to get about $5,000 in cash?

Clerk: _____

7. Refund

Guest: Did you have the late checkout fee taken off my bill?

Clerk: _____

Guest Satisfaction Survey / Handling Complaints

Study the guest satisfaction surveys below.

METROPOLITAN HOTEL

GUEST SATISFACTION SURVEY

NAME (optional)   *Barbara Laporte*

DATES OF STAY   *November 21 – 25*

TEL OR E-MAIL   *b.laporte@gmail.com*

	not satisfied ⟷ very satisfied
Overall Satisfaction	1 - 2 - 3 - ④ - 5
Check-In/Check-Out	1 - 2 - 3 - 4 - ⑤
Guest Room	1 - 2 - 3 - ④ - 5
Hotel Services	1 - 2 - 3 - 4 - ⑤
Hotel Facilities	1 - 2 - ③ - 4 - 5
Food and Beverage	1 - 2 - 3 - 4 - ⑤

Comments

Had a wonderful stay. I was a little disappointed that the day spa was closed for renovations, but your excellent service more than made up for it. Also, your restaurants are all quite excellent, but I especially enjoyed my meal at Bistro Urbana. Thank you so much for everything!

METROPOLITAN HOTEL

GUEST SATISFACTION SURVEY

NAME (optional)   *Dexter McManus*

DATES OF STAY   *11.26 – 11.28*

TEL OR E-MAIL   *0930–355–868*

	not satisfied ←→ very satisfied
Overall Satisfaction	1 - 2 - ③ - 4 - 5
Check-In/Check-Out	1 - 2 - 3 - ④ - 5
Guest Room	1 - ② - 3 - 4 - 5
Hotel Services	1 - 2 - 3 - ④ - 5
Hotel Facilities	① - 2 - 3 - 4 - 5
Food and Beverage	1 - 2 - ③ - 4 - 5

Comments

Your staff is courteous and well trained, but your facilities need to be improved. The pool was out of service and the carpet in my room was stained. You can do better!

Now read the hotel manager's responses. Notice the key phrases for responding to compliments and complaints, which are in bold. With a partner, decide to which guest each reach response is directed. Some responses may be directed to both guests.

1. <u>Mr. McManus</u>   **I'm sorry your stay was** less than satisfactory.

2. <u>Both</u>   **Thank you for taking the time to** respond to our survey.

3. _____   **I'm glad you enjoyed** your stay.

4. _____   **We're committed to** making your next stay even more enjoyable.

5. _____   **I'm truly sorry that** your room was not up to acceptable standards.

6. _____   **I understand how frustrating it can be when** facilities you were planning to use are not available.

7. _____   **We take great pride in our** dining options, so **I was especially happy to know that** you enjoyed your meals at the Metropolitan.

8. _____   Our pool will reopen on December 1. **We'd like to offer you a free upgrade** if you stay with us again before the end of the year.

Role Play

Use the vocabulary and phrases you've practiced in this chapter to act out these scenes.

Scene 1

Guest: You are checking out. You have many complaints about your experience and demand a discount on your bill.

Clerk: A guest is unhappy with the hotel. Apologize to the guest, clarify any problems with the bill, but do not offer any unreasonable discounts.

Scene 2

Guest: You are a famous movie star checking out of the hotel. You are very demanding and require all sorts of special services to ensure your privacy.

Clerk: Help a celebrity check out of the hotel. Answer all of his or her questions, but act quickly as there are many other guests waiting for assistance.

Discussion

Do you agree or disagree with the following statements? Why or why not?

1. _____ Guests should be compensated by the hotel in some way if they did not enjoy their stay.

2. _____ During checkout, agents should spend as much time as possible asking about each guest's stay.

3. _____ VIP guests should be treated much better than regular guests.

Discuss the following questions.

1. What special privileges should be offered to VIP guests? What special services would be considered "asking for too much"?

2. What is the best way to send off a guest? Why?

3. How much importance should hotels place on guest satisfaction surveys? Why?

CHAPTER 08

Review

01 Hotel Reservations

03 The Hotel Room

04 Hotel Services

06 The Gift Shop

07 Checking Out

02 Checking In

05 The Business Center

In this chapter ...

With a partner take turns playing the role of hotel clerk and guest.

Hotel clerk: Complete each task in order before moving on to the next mission. If you get stuck, quickly review the pages listed in each section.

Guest: Look at page 178 for suggestions about how to play your part. If the role play is too easy, feel free to cause some problems!

Mission 1 Take a Reservation

Mission 2 Check In a Guest

Mission 3 Introduce a Hotel Room

Mission 4 Explain the Hotel's Services

Mission 5 Assist a Guest in the Business Center

Mission 6 Sell Something at the Gift Shop

Mission 7 Check Out a Guest

Let's Start!

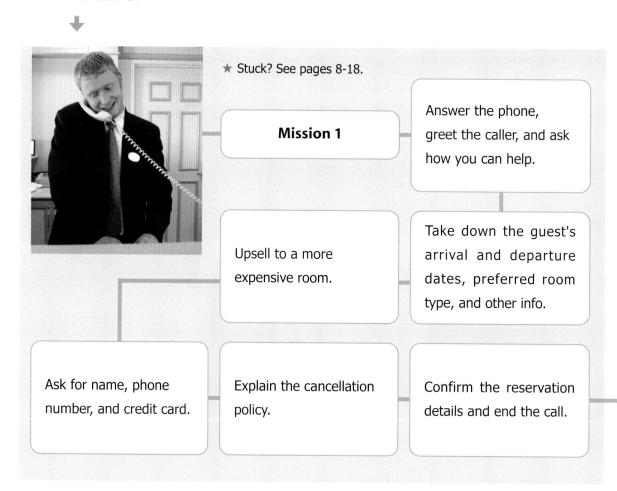

★ Stuck? See pages 8-18.

Mission 1

Answer the phone, greet the caller, and ask how you can help.

Take down the guest's arrival and departure dates, preferred room type, and other info.

Upsell to a more expensive room.

Ask for name, phone number, and credit card.

Explain the cancellation policy.

Confirm the reservation details and end the call.

★ Stuck? See pages 30-40.

Show the guest to his or her room.

Say goodbye.

Mission 3

Tell the guest where things in the room are located.

Ask what else you can do for the guest.

Show the guest how to adjust the thermostat.

Explain the hotel laundry service.

Present the key and assist the guest with his or her luggage.

Ask the guest to sign the registration card.

Request to see the guest's passport and credit card.

Introduce the hotel's restaurants and other facilities.

Confirm the guest's reservation details.

Mission 2

Greet the guest and ask if they are checking in.

★ Stuck? See pages 19-29.

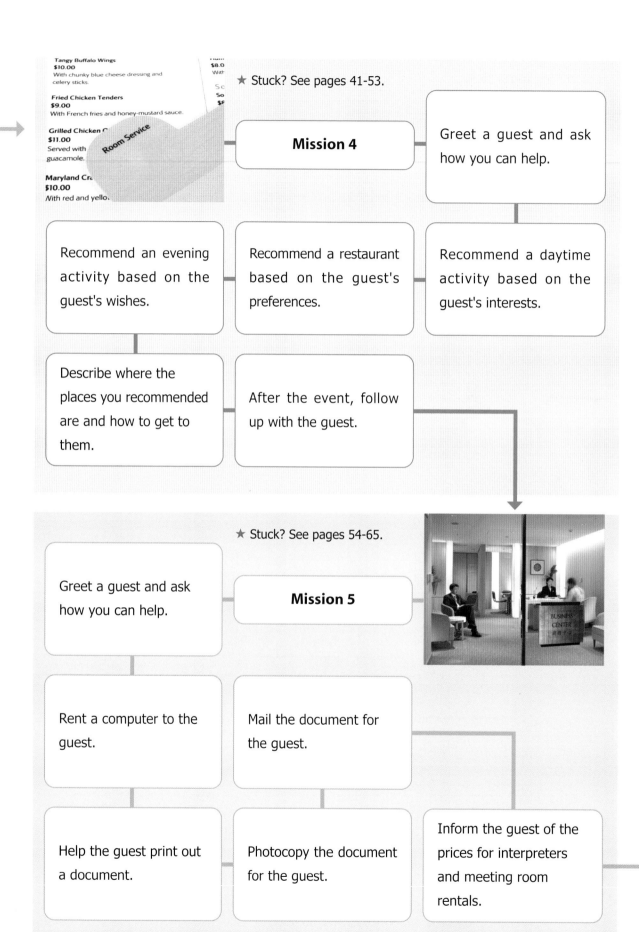

★ Stuck? See pages 41-53.

Mission 4

Greet a guest and ask how you can help.

Recommend an evening activity based on the guest's wishes.

Recommend a restaurant based on the guest's preferences.

Recommend a daytime activity based on the guest's interests.

Describe where the places you recommended are and how to get to them.

After the event, follow up with the guest.

★ Stuck? See pages 54-65.

Greet a guest and ask how you can help.

Mission 5

Rent a computer to the guest.

Mail the document for the guest.

Help the guest print out a document.

Photocopy the document for the guest.

Inform the guest of the prices for interpreters and meeting room rentals.

Offer assistance with luggage and transportation.

See the guest off.

Take a break!

Explain the charges to the guest.

Prepare the bill and ask for payment.

Inquire about the guest's stay.

Mission 7

Greet the guest. Confirm that the guest is checking out.

★ Stuck? See pages 76-86.

See the customer off.

Receive payment and give the customer the change and the receipt.

Compliment the customer.

Mission 6

Offer to assist the customer.

Describe a product and recommend it.

If you don't have an item, suggest where the customer could buy it.

★ Stuck? See pages 66-75.

Part II

Restaurant

CHAPTER 09

Restaurant Reservations

In this chapter ...

■ **Taking Reservations**
Booking tables, asking for guest information, handling reservation changes

■ **Reservations Vocabulary**
Dates and times, common words and phrases for restaurant reservations

■ **Advanced Skills**
Handling special situations and special reservation requests

 **Conversation**

Listen to the conversation and then take turns practicing it with a partner.

H = Host   G = Guest

H Good afternoon, you've reached The Pizzeria. Lizzy speaking, how may I help you?

G Yes, hello. I'd like to book a table for tonight, please.

H Sure. And how many people are coming?

G Eight.

H We include a 10% service charge for parties of six or more. Is that OK with you?

G Yeah, I know. It's fine.

H Great. What time is the reservation for?

G 6:30, if you still have an opening.

H I'm afraid we're fully booked at 6:30, but we do have a table available at 7:00.

G All right, I'll take the table at 7:00, then.

H OK. May I have your name and telephone number, please?

G My name is Jeremy Gould, G - O - U - L - D, and my number is 0945-314-914.

H Thank you, Mr. Gould. Let me repeat your reservation. I've put you down for a table for eight at 7:00.

G That's right, thanks.

H Is there anything else I can help you with?

G Yes, actually. I was wondering if we could get a table outside. Is that possible?

H Certainly. We have a table in the garden that's just big enough for eight.

G Sounds good. Thanks for your help.

H You're welcome. See you tonight, Mr. Gould.

▓ book (*v.*) 預訂（房間、座位等）(= reserve)

▓ service charge 服務費

▓ opening (*n.*) 空位

▓ put down 寫下；把……加入名單

Days, Dates, Months, and Years

Study the table below. Notice when *on* and *in* are used.

Preposition	Time	Examples
on	**Days**	• We're fully booked **on Friday**. • We have a table available **on Wednesday** afternoon.
	Dates	• Sorry, we're full **on May 12**, but we have a table open **on May 13**. • She booked a table for May 11 **on May 10**.
in	**Months**	• If you wanted to eat there this weekend, you should've made a reservation **in February**. • Our restaurant did very well **in January**.
	Years	• The Pizzeria opened its first branch **in 1996**. • Mr. and Mrs. Chen first came to our restaurant **in 1982**, and they've been coming ever since.

Listen and complete the following sentences. Mp3 55

1. The restaurant is full _____, but there's a table available _____.

2. He tried to make a reservation for Friday night _____, but the restaurant was already fully booked.

3. Did you make a reservation at Café Blue for her birthday party _____?

4. They originally wanted a table _____, but we couldn't accommodate them at that time.

5. Unfortunately, we don't have any tables available _____, but we do have a table available _____.

6. Our restaurant opened _____, was redesigned _____, and changed its name _____.

Telling the Time

Guests calling the restaurant may use either the basic or casual form of telling the time, so you have to be prepared to deal with both.

Basic :	It's seven o'clock.
Casual:	It's seven.

Basic :	It's seven ten.
Casual:	It's ten after seven.

Basic :	It's seven fifteen.
Casual:	It's (a) quarter after seven.

Basic :	It's seven thirty.
Casual:	It's half past seven.

Basic :	It's seven forty-five.
Casual:	It's (a) quarter to / of eight.

Basic :	It's seven fifty.
Casual:	It's ten to / of eight.

🎧 Mp3 56

Listen to ten short conversations and write down the time, if any, that the reservation was made for. The first one has been done for you.

1.   7:00   6. _____
2. _____   7. _____
3. _____   8. _____
4. _____   9. _____
5. _____   10. _____

Useful Words and Phrases for Making Reservations

- available 空的
- opening (*n.*) 空位
- party (party of four) 位（四位）
- put sb. down for sth. 幫某人排定某事
- squeeze sb. in 把某人安插進去
- pencil sb. in 把某人登記上去
- push (a reservation) back （把訂位）往後延
- cancellation 取消
- hold a reservation 保留訂位
- fully booked 訂光了
- wait (*n.*) 等待
- put sb. on the waiting list 把某人列入候補名單
- smoking section 吸菸區
- non-smoking section 非吸菸區
- first available 第一順位
- booth （餐廳的）雅座
- quiet table 安靜的桌子
- near the window 靠窗
- away from the kitchen 遠離廚房
- on the patio 在中庭
- al fresco 戶外；露天
- wheelchair accessible 可供輪椅
- high chair 高腳椅（兒童餐椅）
- booster seat 輔助座椅

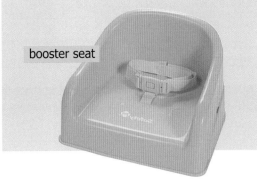

high chair

booster seat

Taking Reservations

Listen to six dialogs and complete the reservations record. 🎧 Mp3 57

1. Make a reservation for Ms. Lemon.
2. Make a reservation for Mr. Marley.
3. Make a reservation for Miss Shirley.
4. Make a reservation for Mr. Lin.
5. Change Mr. Ford's reservation.
6. Make a reservation for Mrs. Wu.

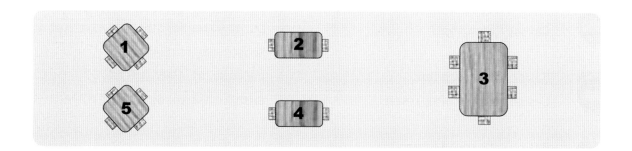

Special   Memory   Diary

Reservations

Time	Name	No. in Party	Table	Notes
6:00	Jones	4	9	table by window
	Saunders	4	13	
	Ford	2	2	needs booster seat
6:30	Kim	5	8	
7:00	Chang	3	10	needs wheelchair access
7:30	Chu	2	12	
8:00	Niven	3	9	
9:00	Garcia	4	13	
	Rounds	2	12	

Valuable

Sentence Patterns

Study and practice these patterns.

Greeting and Offering Assistance

■ **Good [time of day]. [Restaurant name.]**
How may / can I help you?
Good evening. Paris Bistro. **How may I help you?**
Good afternoon. New York Deli. **How can I help you?**

Taking a Reservation

■ **What time ...?**
What time is the reservation for?
What time can we expect you?

■ **How many ...?**
How many is the reservation for?
How many in your party?

Getting Contact Information

■ **May I have your ...?**
May I have your name, please?
May I have your telephone number, please?

Clarifying Information

■ **Could you + V ...?**
Could you repeat your telephone number, please?
Could you spell your name, please?

Checking and Confirming Reservation Details

■ **Let me + V ....**
Let me see if we have anything available at that time.
Let me repeat your reservation.

Ending the Call

■ **Thank you for ....**
Thank you for calling.
Thank you for your reservation.

■ **Is there anything else ...?**
Is there anything else I can help you with?
Is there anything else I can do for you?

When the Restaurant Is Fully Booked

■ **Sorry, we + V ....**
Sorry, we're full on Tuesday.
Sorry, we're fully booked this weekend.
Sorry, we don't have any tables available tonight.

Suggesting an Alternative Time

■ **We have a + N ....**
We have a table available at 7:30, though.
We have an opening tomorrow evening.

Changing or Canceling a Reservation

■ **What time ...?**
What time shall I put you down for?
What time would you like to change the reservation to?

■ **I have + Ved ....**
I've canceled your reservation.
I've changed your reservation to 1:00.

Guests with Special Needs

■ **We provide / have ....**
We provide high chairs for young children.
We have booster seats for kids.

■ **The restaurant is ....**
The restaurant is wheelchair accessible.

Accommodating Special Requests

■ **I can / will + V ....**
I can add two chairs for you, if you'd like.
I can add your name to the waiting list, if you'd like.
I'll ask the chef to prepare a special dessert.
I'll reserve a table next to the window for you.
I'll take care of that for you.

 **Listening**

Listen and complete these conversations.

H = Host   G = Guest

1 Canceling a Reservation   Mp3 58

H Good afternoon. Coco Café. _____?

G Hi. I made a reservation for _____ people tonight, but now we'll have _____.

H Let me _____ a larger table available at that time. May I have your
_____, please?

G My name's Jennifer Goodman, and my number is _____.

H Thank you. OK. I see that you made a reservation for _____.

G Yeah, that's right.

H Unfortunately, we don't have _____ for six people at that time.

G You don't? Can't you just add two chairs?

H No, I'm afraid not. But we do _____ at 8:30.

G No, that won't do. We're going to see a movie at 9:00.

H Oh, I'm sorry. I can add your name _____, if you'd like.

G I don't think that will be necessary. Thanks anyway.

H I'm sorry about that. I've _____ for this evening. Is there
_____ I can help you with?

G No, I think that's it.

H All right, thank you _____, Ms. Goodman.

2 Special Requests   Mp3 59

■ Changing a reservation

H Good morning. Tokyo Bar and Grill. _____?

G I'd like to _____. I've got a table at _____, but I'm going to
be a little late. Could you push it back to _____?

H Sorry, we're full then. We _____, though. I could _____ then. Is that OK?

■ Special seating arrangements

G Hi, I was wondering if your restaurant is _____.

H Yes, it is. Just take the elevator on the south side of the lobby. We can arrange a table
near the entrance.

G That's great. I was also wondering if you have _____.

H Oh, I'm sorry, we don't. But we do have _____. Would that be OK?

■ **Adding chairs**

G I'd like a table for five at 6:30 tonight.

H _____ we have anything available at that time.... Unfortunately, we only have a table _____.

G Isn't there a way to fit us all in?

H Hmm. _____ another chair for you, if you'd like. It might be a little crowded, though.

G Oh, that's fine. Thank you so much!

When the Restaurant Is Fully Booked

Use the sentences below to complete this conversation between a host and a guest.

1. _____ Never mind, then. I'll try somewhere else. Thanks.

2. _____ All right, thank you for calling.

3. _____ Bistro Shangri-La. How can I help you?

4. _____ OK, that's fine. Put me down for the six o'clock table, please.

5. _____ I'm sorry, we're all booked at seven fifteen. But we have a table available at six.

A

↓

Can I get a table for four tomorrow night at seven fifteen, please?

↓

B

↓ ↓

Oh, no, that's much too early. What about nine? Do you have a table open at nine?	C

↓ ↓

I'm afraid not, sorry	Great. May I have your name and phone number, please?

↓ ↓

D	Sure. My name is Harry Crawford, that's C-R-A-W-F-O-R-D, and my number is 0922-901-832.

↓

E

Handling Special Requests

Use the sentences below to complete this conversation between a host and a guest.

1. _____ Yes, I want to book a table for sixteen people. Is that possible?

2. _____ Oh, definitely the garden area. Thanks.

3. _____ Well, we'll be celebrating my husband's fiftieth birthday, so I'm wondering if the restaurant offers any special treats for birthdays.

4. _____ Yes, that's perfectly possible. Would you like to be seated in the garden area or inside the main dining hall?

5. _____ Well, we only allow parties of ten or fewer. I can, however, book two tables of eight for you.

6. _____ Yes, we do. I'll ask the chef to prepare a special dessert.

Bistro Shangri-La. How can I help you?

⬇

A

⬇   ⬇

B   **C**

⬇   ⬇

That's fine with me. Thank you so much.   **D**

⬇

Great. May I have your name and number?

⬇

My name's Ivy Chang, and my telephone number is 0939-863-218.

⬇

Thank you very much, Ms. Chang. Is there anything else I can help you with?

⬇

E

⬇

F

Role Play

Use the vocabulary and phrases you've practiced in this chapter to act out the scene.

Guest: Call a restaurant to make reservation. Before hanging up, change the time of the reservation, the number of people the reservation is for, and make two or three special requests.

Host: Answer the phone and take a reservation. Be patient and calm. Try not to let the guest know that there is a fire in the kitchen and the restaurant is being evacuated.

Discussion

Do you agree or disagree with the following statements? Why or why not?

1. _____ Restaurants that require reservations are always better than restaurants that don't.

2. _____ A host should do everything in his or her power to help a customer—even if the customer is being unreasonable.

3. _____ The role of the host will become less and less important as online reservations become more common.

4. _____ The best way to tell if a restaurant is good is to see how many people are eating there.

5. _____ The best way to celebrate your birthday is to have a meal with family and friends at your favorite restaurant.

Interview a Classmate

1. What's your favorite cuisine? Your least favorite? Why?

2. What's your favorite food? Your least favorite? Why?

3. What's the strangest thing you've ever eaten? Did you enjoy it?

4. What's your favorite "comfort food"? Explain.

5. What's your favorite restaurant? Why do you like it?

6. What restaurant would you take a date to? What about your parents? Your significant other's parents? Your boss? Your foreign friends?

7. It is said that "one should eat to live, not live to eat." Do you agree? Why or why not?

CHAPTER 10

Welcoming and Seating

In this chapter ...

Greeting Guests
Welcoming guests, requesting reservation details, placing guests on the waiting list

Seating Guests
Inquiring about guest preferences, assigning tables, staff self-introductions

Vocabulary
Restaurant employees, common buffet terms

Advanced Skills
Handling special situations and complaints, explanations of buffet policies

Conversation

Listen to the conversation and then take turns practicing it with a partner.

H = Hostess   G = Guest

H Hi, welcome to D'Angelo's. How can I help you?

G Hi. We'd like a table for two.

H Do you have a reservation?

G No, we don't.

H I'm sorry. We don't have any tables available at the moment. Would you mind sitting at the bar?

G I think we'd prefer a table in the dining area, if possible. How long is the wait?

H 20 to 30 minutes.

G Oh, never mind, then. I'll take the bar seats.

H Great. Let me show you to your seats. This way, please.

G Thanks.

H Is this your first time here?

G Yes, it is.

H Well, we're most famous for our buffet. The cold dishes are there on the left, and the hot ones are on the right. Desserts are in the corner and an unlimited number of drinks are included. We also have an excellent à la carte menu, of course, which you're also welcome to order from.

G All right, thanks.

H You're welcome. Here are your menus. Your server will be here in just a moment to take your order. Enjoy your meal!

▓ dining area 用餐區

▓ buffet [buˋfe] *n.* 自助餐

▓ desserts [dɪˋzɜt] *n.* 甜點

▓ unlimited [ʌnˋlɪmɪtɪd] *adj.* 無限制的

▓ à la carte 單點菜

Employee Titles

Host / Hostess   Sommelier   Server   Bartender   Cashier   Busboy   Kitchen staff   Manager   Head chef

Match each job title with its responsibilities.

■ Responsibilities

_____ **A.** making dishes, cleaning

_____ **B.** supervising restaurant operations

_____ **C.** setting and clearing tables

_____ **D.** making drinks

_____ **E.** taking reservations, seating guests

_____ **F.** taking and serving food orders

_____ **G.** handling the wine service

_____ **H.** managing the cash register

_____ **I.** overseeing the kitchen, making dishes

Complete the sentences.

1. I can't decide what to order. Let's ask the _____ for some recommendations.

(A) waiter   (B) busboy   (C) cashier

2. The _____ apologized to the woman for the worm in her salad and offered her a full refund.

(A) sommelier   (B) manager   (C) hostess

3. Could you ask the _____ to double-check the bill, please? I think she overcharged us.

(A) cashier   (B) busgirl   (C) chef

4. Because it was my birthday, the _____ made a special cocktail for me.

(A) bartender   (B) sommelier   (C) seating host

5. The _____ accidentally dropped a knife while he was clearing the table.

(A) host   (B) kitchen staff   (C) busperson

Introducing the Buffet

Identify these common buffet foods.

- ham _____
- fried rice _____
- salami _____
- fried noodles _____
- sushi _____

- salad dressing _____
- pizza _____
- grapefruit _____
- croissant _____
- sashimi _____

- roast beef _____
- pasta salad _____
- cheese _____
- oysters _____

Complete the description with words from the box. Check your answers by listening to the talk.

🎧 Mp3 61

Foods	Drinks	Adjectives
seafood	beverages	hot
salad	tea	cold
sandwich	hot chocolate	fresh
desserts	coffee	famous
breads	juice	excellent

Our buffet is _____ for the variety and quality of the food. I think you'll soon see why. On the left, we have the _____ section, where you can get everything from an ice-_____ grapefruit _____ to a steaming _____ or _hot chocolate_. We even have an automatic espresso machine for _____ lovers.

On your right, you can see our _____ bar, where we offer eight types of dressing. And just beyond it is our _____ station where you can make your own masterpiece with _____ baked _____ each morning in our own bakery, cheeses from around the world, and deli meats, such as ham and salami.

The _____ section is right beside the salads, and it's where you will find our sushi, sashimi and oysters. The _____ foods are located near the back. We offer pasta, pizza, roast beef, and an Asian section with fried rice and noodles. Last but certainly not least is the _____ section. Our French pastry chef makes everything fresh each morning. Our chocolate croissants are truly_____ , so be sure to try one before you leave!

Assigning Tables

Study the floor plan below, and then mark the table where each of the following guests should sit.

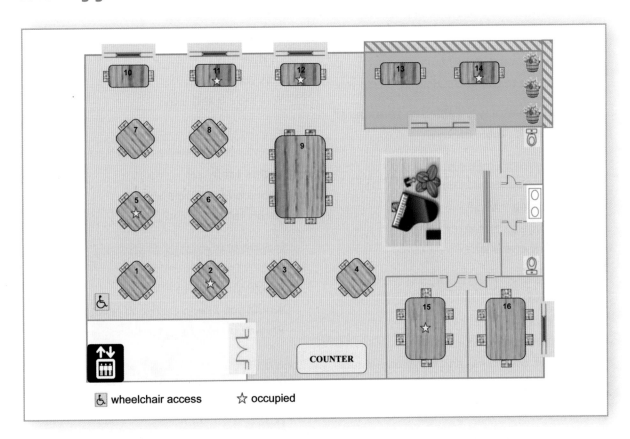

Name	Table	Party of	Notes
Mr. Watanabe	No. ____	4	needs a table with wheelchair access
Miss Pearce	No. ____	2	prefers to sit near the window
Mrs. Luca	No. ____	1	wants to dine on the balcony
Mr. Gomez	No. ____	6	requests a private area to talk business
Mr. Lai	No. ____	3	requests a table near the bathroom
Miss Zhao	No. ____	4	wants a table near the exit

Sentence Patterns

Study and practice these patterns.

Greeting Guests

- **Hello, welcome to ....**
  Hello, welcome to the Pizzeria.
  Hi, welcome to D'Angelo's. How can I help you?

- **Good [time of day]. Table for [number]?**
  Good evening. **Table for** two?

Checking for Reservations

- **Do / Did you + V ...?**
  Do you have a reservation?
  Did you reserve a table?

Getting Reservation Details

- **May / Can I + V ...?**
  May I have your name, please?
  Can I get your name and telephone number, please?

Putting Guests on the Waiting List

- **Would you like ...?**
  Would you like to wait?
  Would you like me to put you on the waiting list?
  Would you like us to call you when a table opens up?

Announcing a Guest's Table Is Ready

- **... your table is ready.**
  Sir, **your table is ready**.
  Wu, party of three, **your table is ready**.

Leading Guests to the Table

- **Please + V ....**
  Please come with me.
  Please follow me to your table.

  Please let me show you to your table.
  Please sit anywhere you like.

- **... this way ....**
  This way, please.
  Your table is **this way**.

Confirming Satisfaction

- **Is this table ...?**
  Is this table OK with you?
  Is this table all right?

Offering an Alternative

- **Would you like to + V ...?**
  Would you like to change to another table?
  Would you like to switch tables?

Presenting Menus

- **Here is / are ....**
  Here is the menu.
  Here are your menus.

Introducing the Waiter

- **Your waiter ....**
  Your waiter will be with you in just a moment.
  Your waiter tonight will be Sherrie, and she'll be here in just a moment.

Waiter Self-introduction

- **Hi, I'm ... and I'll be ....**
  Hi, I'm Mary, **and I'll be** your server tonight.
  Hi, I'm John, **and I'll be** taking care of you this evening.

 **Listening**

Listen to the questions and choose the correct response to each.

🎧 Mp3 62

1. ☐ Hi, I've got a reservation for three at 8 o'clock.

   ☐ I'd like the roast beef, please.

   ☐ Could we get the bill?

2. ☐ May I have your name and telephone number, please?

   ☐ This way, please.

   ☐ Chou, party of two? Yes, your table is ready.

3. ☐ No, but would you like me to put you on the waiting list?

   ☐ Watanabe, party of four?

   ☐ Welcome to Suzuki Sushi!

4. ☐ This way to your table, please.

   ☐ May I have your name, please?

   ☐ No, I'm afraid we're full at the moment.

5. ☐ Yes, please follow me.

   ☐ Yes. Is it all right with you?

   ☐ Yes, let me show you to your table.

Listen and complete the following conversations.

G = Guest H = Hostess / Host

1 🎧 Mp3 63

   G Do you have a table for four, by any chance?

   H Sorry, _____, but would you like me to call you _____?

   G Yeah, that sounds good, thanks.

   H Great. _____ and telephone number, please?

   G Yes, my name is Goddard, and my number is 0930-765-514.

   H Could you _____, please?

   G Yeah, it's G-O-D-D-A-R-D.

   H OK, thanks. I'll call you _____, Mr. Goddard.

2 🎧 Mp3 64

> **G** Could you please check if our table is ready yet?
>
> **H** Sure. _____, please?
>
> **G** Goddard. G-O-D-D-A-R-D.
>
> **H** Goddard, _____?
>
> **G** Yes, that's right.
>
> **H** Yes, your table is ready. _____.

3 🎧 Mp3 65

> **H** _____?
>
> **G** Yes, it's fine.
>
> **H** All right. _____ menus. _____ tonight will be James, and he'll _____ in just a moment.
>
> **G** Thank you very much.
>
> **H** Enjoy your evening.

 # Special Situations and Problems

How would you respond to the customer requests listed below? Practice both positive and negative responses with your partner. Use the phrases in the box, and make up one or two of your own.

Positive	Negative
A. Sure, no problem.	**a.** I'm sorry, that table is reserved.
B. Of course, I'd be happy to.	**b.** I'm sorry, but we don't have any other tables available.
C. Please go ahead.	**c.** I'm very sorry, but there's really nothing I can do about that.
D. OK, how about this table?	
E. Yes, I'll take care of that right away.	**d.** I'm sorry, it's the restaurant's policy.
F. Let me check with the manager about that.	
G. _____	**e.** _____
H. _____	**f.** _____

1. _____ Can we have that table by the window?

2. _____ Is it OK if we sit in the booth?

3. _____ Could we sit over here instead?

4. _____ We'd rather not sit next to the kitchen.

5. _____ Do you have a table that's not so close to the air conditioner?

6. _____ Could we have some water, please?

7. _____ We need another place setting.

8. _____ Could you give us another menu?

9. _____ Could you bring me a new napkin? I just dropped mine on the floor.

10. _____ It's a little hot in here. Could you turn on the air conditioner?

11. _____ I'm a little cold. Is there any way you could turn down the air conditioner?

12. _____ It's too dark to read the menu. Do you have a candle or a flashlight or something?

13. _____ Could you close the blinds? It's getting a little bright in here.

14. _____ Could you turn the music down a little bit?

15. _____ Could you ask that couple to take their kid outside until he stops crying?

16. _____ Isn't this supposed to be a non-smoking restaurant?

17. _____ What do you mean I can't smoke here?

18. _____ Could we move to another table please?

19. _____ Could you ask the table over there to keep it down?

20. _____ The guy at the next table is drunk. Is there anything you can do?

 ## Problems at the Buffet

Practice these conversations with a partner and then answer the questions below.

G = Guest   S = Server

1. Commenting on dish availability

G You're out of shrimp again.

S I see. Well, we bring out a new plate every 15 minutes.

G 15 minutes? Are you afraid we're going to eat it all?

S No, we just want to make sure everything is fresh.

2. Explaining the time limit

S I'm sorry, but we have a two-hour limit.

G What do you mean? Doesn't the restaurant close at 10:00?

S Yes, but we have a two-hour time limit per table. You're welcome to stay for another half hour, however.

3. Asking for payment

S I'm sorry, but our cashier needs to close out the register. Could I ask you to pay the bill first, please?

G Oh, right. Of course.

S Thank you very much, ma'am.

4. Preparing guests for closing time

S Excuse me. I just wanted to let you know that we're going to start cleaning up in about half hour, so if you'd like another serving, please help yourself.

G So soon? I just got here two hours ago.

S Well, the drink bar will be open for another half hour, so take your time. And please let me know when you're ready for the check.

Questions for Discussion

1. How well did the server handle each of these situations?

2. Would you have handled them differently? If so, how?

3. What other situations might a server at a buffet restaurant encounter? How would you handle those situations?

 # Role Play

Use the vocabulary and phrases you've practiced in this chapter to act out these scenes.

Host: Take down a guest's reservation details.

Guest: Keep changing your mind about what time you'll arrive and how many people will be coming.

Hostess: Show a guest to his or her seat.

Guest: You're unsatisfied with your table and want to switch to another (and another … and another…).

Manager: Take a VIP guest on a tour of the restaurant.

Guest: You're a VIP, and curious about what each restaurant employee does, and also about each of the dishes served at the buffet.

 # Design Your Own Restaurant

Together with a few classmates, design a layout for your own restaurant. Use the following questions as a guide. When you're done, present your ideas to the class.

❖ What kind of food would you serve?

❖ Where is your restaurant located? Does it have a view?

❖ What facilities does your restaurant have? Waiting area? Bar? Buffet? Private rooms?

❖ How many diners does your restaurant accommodate?

❖ Is the ambience intimate or open?

❖ How would you decorate the restaurant?

❖ What kind of staff would you need? What kind of uniforms would they wear?

CHAPTER 11

Taking Orders

In this chapter ...

■ **Introducing the Menu**
Describing cooking methods, flavors, and textures

■ **Taking Orders**
Appetizers, soups, salads, main courses, and beverages

■ **Advanced Skills**
Making recommendations and handling problems

 # Conversation

Listen to the conversation and then take turns practicing it with a partner.

G = Guest   S = Server

G Excuse me. We're ready to order.

S I'll be with you in just a minute. … Sorry to keep you waiting. Would you care for an appetizer this evening?

G No, thank you, but I do have a question about the Coq au Vin. Is it fried?

S The chicken is sautéed, but only briefly. After that, it's cooked very slowly in a red wine sauce with bacon, herbs, and fresh vegetables.

G That sounds tempting.

S Yes, and the chicken is quite tender. Coq au Vin is our chef's specialty.

G OK. I'll have that.

S Sure. That comes with your choice of rice pilaf or baked potatoes.

G The potatoes, please.

S And what kind of soup would you like? We have cream of mushroom, French onion, and pumpkin.

G The pumpkin sounds good.

S Pumpkin soup. And what kind of salad dressing would you like?

G Do you have Thousand Island?

S Yes, we do. And can I get you something to drink? Some wine or beer?

G I'll take an iced tea, if you have it.

S We sure do. Let me repeat your order. That's Coq au Vin with baked potatoes, pumpkin soup, a garden salad with Thousand Island, and an iced tea.

G That's right.

S OK, thank you very much. I'll be right back with your tea. If you need anything at all tonight, just let me know.

G Thank you.

▓ Coq au Vin *n.* 紅葡萄酒雞

▓ sautéed [soˋted] *v.* 嫩煎

▓ herb [hɝb] *n.* 草本植物

▓ tempting [ˋtɛmptɪŋ] *adj.* 吸引人的

▓ tender [ˋtɛndɚ] *adj.* 嫩的

▓ specialty [ˋspɛʃəltɪ] *n.* 主廚的拿手菜

▓ rice pilaf *n.* 調味炒飯

▓ Thousand Island *n.* 千島（醬）

Describing Cooking Methods

Sort these cooking methods into the boxes below.

bake	simmer	poach	broil
stir fry	boil	sautée	roast
steam	smoke	deep fry	braise

Oven/Grill	Water	Oil

With your partner, use the words above to translate these Chinese dishes.

■ 紅燒蹄膀
braised pork knuckles with soy sause

■ 清蒸魚
_____

■ 炸雞
_____

■ 烤鮭魚
_____

■ 水煮玉米
_____

■ 清炒時蔬
_____

 # Describing Flavors and Textures

Fill in the blanks with a flavor or texture you associate with the food or dish.

Flavors : spicy / rich / tangy / creamy / mild
Textures : crispy / tender/ juicy / smooth / moist

kung pao chicken

chinese rice porridge

beef stew

steak

juicy

muffin

sweet and sour pork

pasta alfredo

potato chips

mashed potatoes

cheese cake

 Describing Dishes

Work with a partner to identify the following common Chinese dishes.

1. Pork and vegetable dumplings, braised then wok-fried. Served with soy sauce, vinegar, and chili sauce for dipping. _____

2. Juicy pieces of deep-fried pork stir fried with bell peppers, onions, carrots, and pineapple in a tangy sweet and sour sauce. _____

3. Chicken with peanuts stir fried in a spicy chili sauce. Topped with fresh green onions and served with steamed rice. _____

Read the following menu item and answer the questions.

Murgh Shahi Korma

Tender pieces of boneless chicken breast, gently simmered with Indian spices and a mild cashew yoghurt sauce. Served with fresh, seasonal vegetables and steamed rice.

1. What is the name of the dish? _____

2. What is the main ingredient? _____

3. How is the dish prepared? _____

4. What is the dish served with? _____

Most menu descriptions include some if not all of the four elements above. Now practice describing the following dishes to a partner.

1. Beef Lasagna 牛肉千層麵   **2.** Peking Duck 北京烤鴨   **3.** Bibimbap 石鍋拌飯

Conversation Practice

Using the menu below, practice ordering a meal with a partner. Note any difficulties that you have.

MENU

Appetizers

★ Shrimp Cocktail   ★ Buffalo Wings

Soups and Salads

★ Minestrone   ★ Pumpkin Soup

★ Garden Salad   ★ Caesar Salad

Entrées

Roast Beef

Three juicy slices of roast beef. Served with your choice of baked, mashed, or french fried potatoes.

Coq au Vin

Tender breast of chicken cooked slowly in a rich burgundy wine sauce with mushrooms and fresh herbs. Accompanied with fresh pasta and vegetables.

Pasta Primavera

Mushrooms, broccoli, and peas sautéed in garlic and a light cream sauce. Served over the pasta of your choice and topped with parmesan cheese and pine nuts.

Beverages

★ Coffee   ★ Tea   ★ Lemonade

★ Coke   ★ Beer   ★ Wine

Desserts

Black Forest Cake

Tiramisu Cheesecake

Apple Crisp

15% service charge automatically added to parties of six or more.

Cash, traveler's checks, MasterCard, Visa and American Express accepted.

Sentence Patterns

Study and practice these patterns.

Making a Suggestion

■ **Would you care for ...?**
Would you care for something to drink?

■ **Can I + V ...?**
Can I get you some ketchup for your fries?

Explaining a Service

■ **We have ....**
We have orange juice, apple juice, and grape juice.

■ **That comes with + N.**
That comes with a dinner salad.

Offering Choices

■ **Would you like N or N?**
Would you like coffee **or** tea?

■ **Would you like (it) Adj. or Adj.?**
Would you like the fish steamed **or** fried?

■ **... either ... or ....**
That comes with **either** rice pilaf **or** a baked potato.

Determining Preferences

■ **What kind of ...?**
What kind of salad dressing would you like?

■ **How would you like ...?**
How would you like your steak?

Taking Action

■ **I'll + be ....**
I'll be with you in just a minute.
I'll be right back with your soup.

■ **Let me + V ....**
Let me bring you another one right away.

Apologizing

■ **Sorry to + V ....**
Sorry to keep you waiting.

■ **I'm (so) sorry about + N**
I'm so sorry about that.

Repeating and Clarifying

■ **Let me + V ....**
Let me repeat your order.

■ **That's ....**
That's a pasta primavera, minestrone soup, and a lemonade with no ice.

Customer Service

■ **Thank you ....**
Thank you very much for your order.

■ **If you need anything ....**
If you need anything else, just let me know.

 **Listening**

Listen and complete these conversations.

G = Guest   S = Server

1 Are You Ready to Order? 🎧 Mp3 67

■ **Asking for more time**

G Excuse me. We're ready to order.

S I'll _____ in just a minute.

G Sure.

S Sorry _____ waiting. What would you like?

■ **Giving the guest more time**

S Are you ready to order?

G Umm …

S Need _____ minutes?

G Yeah, I think so.

S Take your time. Just _____ when you're ready to order.

2 Ordering Appetizers 🎧 Mp3 68

S Can I _____ to start with, madam?

G No, thank you.

S And how about you sir? Would you _____ an appetizer this evening?

3 Ordering Soup and Salad 🎧 Mp3 69

S Would you like soup or salad _____?

G No, thanks.

S Well, the meal _____ your choice of soup or salad.

G Oh. Well, what kind of soup do you have?

S Our _____ is French onion.

G OK, maybe I'll have a salad.

S Sure. _____ of dressing would you like on your salad? _____ French, Italian, Thousand Island, and ranch.

G I'll have Italian, but could I get it _____?

S Of course.

123

> **S** _____ the salmon pan-fried or grilled?
>
> **G** Grilled.
>
> **S** And _____ the potatoes? Mashed, baked, or fried?
>
> **G** Mashed.

> **S** Would you like _____?
>
> **G** I'd like some tea, please.
>
> **S** Would you like your tea _____ or after?
>
> **G** After.
>
> **S** And for you sir?
>
> **G** What kind of juice do you have?
>
> **S** _____ orange juice, apple juice, and grape juice.
>
> **G** Well, I'll just have a Pepsi.
>
> **S** I'm sorry, _____. Is Coke OK?

 # Making Recommendations

Use these patterns to suggest a dish to a guest.

1. **If you like** seafood, **then you might like our** grilled sea bass with mango sauce.
2. **A lot of people like our** grilled sea bass with mango sauce.
3. **My personal favorite is the** grilled sea bass with mango sauce.
4. **Our** grilled sea bass with mango sauce **is excellent**.
5. **We're famous for our** grilled sea bass with mango sauce.
6. Grilled sea bass with mango sauce **is our chef's specialty**.

Practice these conversations with a partner.

1. **Guest:** What do you recommend?

   Server: (filet mignon) _____

2. **Guest:** Are there any local specialties that you'd suggest?

   Server: (stinky tofu) _____

3. **Guest:** Do you have something that's not too oily?

   Server: (vegetable stew) _____

4. **Guest:** What do you have that's kind of light?

   Server: (sandwich-salad combo) _____

5. **Guest:** We're in a bit of a hurry. Is there something we could get quickly?

   Server: (steamed dumplings) _____

6. **Guest:** Do you have any specials tonight?

   Server: (baked chicken) _____

 ## Handling Problems

Which of these problems have you encountered? If you were the server, how would you handle them? Use the customer service flow chart on the next page to practice your responses.

- ☐ The server brings you the wrong order.
- ☐ You realize you don't have enough money to pay for the meal.
- ☐ There's a fly (or hair) in your soup.
- ☐ You've waited a long time and there's still no food!
- ☐ The food is terrible ... not hot enough, too salty, etc.
- ☐ The restaurant is out of an item.
- ☐ The people at the next table are too loud.
- ☐ The restaurant is too hot or too cold.
- ☐ The server forgot to bring your drink.
- ☐ The tableware is not clean.
- ☐ You were charged for something you didn't order.

Customer Service Flow Chart

Confirm Situation   "There's some lipstick on your glass?"

Apologize   "I'm so sorry about that."

Take Action   "Let me bring you a new one right away."

Make Amends   "There won't be any charge for your drinks tonight."

Follow Up   "Can I get you another refill?"

 ## Role Play

Act out the following situation with a few partners. Use the menu on page 121.

Server: It's your first day on the job and you have a terrible memory.

Guest 1: You're starving, but you don't have a lot of money on you.

Guest 2: You're starving, but you're on a strict diet.

Guest 3: You're a famous chef who has very specific ideas about how your meal should be prepared.

Change partners and try again. This time add one (or more!) of the problems on page 125.

 ## Discussion

Do you agree or disagree with the following statements? Why or why not?

1. _____ The customer is always right.

2. _____ Foreign guests don't usually like to try local foods.

3. _____ Foreign guests should always be provided with a knife and fork instead of chopsticks.

4. _____ It's OK to accept a tip if a guest insists on giving one to you.

5. _____ If guests accidentally order things they cannot eat, they should still pay for them.

6. _____ You can know a lot about a person from the way he or she treats the servers.

Discuss the following questions.

1. What three foods would you recommend all foreign visitors to Taiwan try?

2. If you were working at a Chinese restaurant, what would you recommend to a guest who doesn't like Chinese food?

3. How would you communicate with a guest who doesn't speak Mandarin or English?

4. Where's the best place to get Taiwanese food in your city?

5. What's the best international restaurant in your city?

6. If your friends wanted to open a restaurant, what kind of restaurant would you suggest they open?

CHAPTER 12

Serving and Checking In

In this chapter ...

■ Serving and Checking In on Guests
Presenting dishes, offering additional assistance

■ Advanced Skills
Clearing tables, offering extra items, reviewing the dining experience

■ Vocabulary
Tableware, desserts, coffees, teas

Conversation

🎧 Mp3 72

Listen to the conversation and then take turns practicing it with a partner.

S = Server   G = Guest

S   Are you finished with your appetizer?

G   Yeah, I think so.

S   Let me take some of these dishes away.

G   Thanks.

S   The vegetarian sandwich is for the gentleman.

G   Yes, that's right.

S   Here you go, sir. Be careful. The plate's really hot.

G   Oh, wow. It looks great!

S   Thank you. I'll tell the chef you said that! And who ordered the chicken burger?

G   My son did.

S   OK. Here's your burger, and here's some ketchup and mustard for the fries. Who had the shrimp salad?

G   That would be my mother. She's sitting there. My wife just took her to the restroom.

S   OK. Please tell her the dressing is on the side, and the cocktail sauce is for the shrimp.

G   All right. Is my wife's chicken pie ready yet?

S   No, sorry. It takes a bit longer to bake the pie, but it should be ready in about 10 minutes.

G   OK, I'll let her know.

S   Thanks for your patience. Is there anything else I can get you?

G   Yes, actually. I'd like a few more napkins.

S   More napkins. Of course! Would you like a refill, by the way?

G   Yes, that would be great. Thanks.

S   No problem. I'll be right back with some napkins and your refill.

▓ appetizer [ˈæpəˌtaɪzɚ] *n.* 開胃菜

▓ vegetarian [ˌvɛdʒəˈtɛrɪən] *adj.* 素食的

▓ ketchup [ˈkɛtʃəp] *n.* 調味番茄醬

▓ mustard [ˈmʌstɚd] *n.* 芥末

▓ shrimp [ʃrɪmp] *n.* 蝦

▓ cocktail sauce 雞尾酒醬

▓ napkin [ˈnæpkɪn] *n.* 餐巾

▓ refill [riˈfɪl] *v.* 加水；續杯

Tableware

Work with a partner to identify the items below, and list them in the order they should be placed on the table.

③ _____
④ _____
⑤ _____
⑥ _____
⑦ _____
⑧ _____
⑨ _____
⑩ _____
⑪ _____
⑫ _____
⑬ _____
⑭ _____

❶ _____   ❷ _____

Coffee and Tea

Types of Coffee	Coffee Tools	Coffee with ...
regular 招牌	mug 馬克杯	sugar 糖
decaf 低咖啡因	cup 杯子	artificial sweetener 代糖
black 黑（咖啡）	saucer 茶托；淺碟	(steamed) milk （熱）牛奶
fresh-ground 現磨	demitasse 小咖啡杯	milk foam 奶泡
French roast 法式烘焙	coffee stirrer 咖啡匙	cream 奶油
blend 綜合	coffee maker 咖啡壺	half-and-half 兩者各半
instant 即溶	coffee filter 咖啡濾紙	whipped cream 鮮奶油

Identify these coffee drinks by their ingredients.

① ___Espresso___   ② _____   ③ _____

④ _____   ⑤ _____   ⑥ _____

Useful Phrases when Serving Coffee

Basic Questions

- Are you ready for some coffee?
- Would you like it hot or iced?
- Regular or decaf?
- How do you take your coffee?
- Would you like cream or sugar with that?
- Would you like it with your meal or after?

Asking about Refills

- Would you like a refill?
- More coffee?
- Care for another cup of coffee?
- Can I warm that up for you?

Useful Phrases when Serving Tea

- Would you like Chinese tea, black tea, or herbal tea?
- We have Earl Grey, Darjeeling, oolong, and green tea.
- Yes, we have decaffeinated black tea.
- Would you like your tea hot or iced?
- Do you take milk and sugar with your tea?
- Would you like a slice of lemon with your tea?
- Could I get you some more hot water for your tea?

Sort the teas in the box into the categories below.

① Ceylon	⑧ Lady Grey
② chamomile	⑨ lavender
③ Darjeeling	⑩ oolong
④ Earl Grey	⑪ orange
⑤ English breakfast	⑫ peppermint
⑥ green tea	⑬ pu'er
⑦ jasmine	⑭ rosehip

East Asia ⑥ _____

South Asia _____

Herbal _____

The Dessert Menu

Use the phrases and menu below to practice offering and ordering desserts. Review the phrases on page 124, and use them in your role play.

Dessert

❖ **Black Forest Cake** … $ 50

A rich chocolate cake with black cherries, whipped cream, and chocolate shavings

❖ **Tiramisu** … $ 60

Lady fingers soaked in espresso, covered in mascarpone, and dusted with cocoa powder

❖ **Apple Pie** … $ 60

Crisp apple slices baked in a crispy pie crust and topped with a scoop of vanilla ice cream

Dessert

❖ **Crème Brûlée** … $ 65

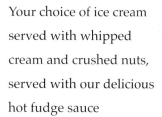
Our famous soft custard in a caramel shell, available in vanilla, coffee, and chocolate

❖ **Ice Cream Sundae** … $ 90

Your choice of ice cream served with whipped cream and crushed nuts, served with our delicious hot fudge sauce

* Ice cream flavors: vanilla, chocolate, and strawberry

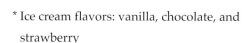

How to Encourage Guests to Have Dessert

❖ Did you save any room for dessert?
❖ Would you care for some dessert?
❖ Would you like to see the menu again?
❖ Would you like to see the dessert tray?
❖ How about some black forest cake?

Sentence Patterns

Study and practice these patterns.

Informing Guests about a Wait

■ **The [dish name] takes ....**
The apple pie **takes** about fifteen minutes to prepare. Is that OK?
Sorry, the crème brûlée **takes** a little longer to make.

Announcing You Will Bring Something

■ **I'll be right back with ....**
I'll be right back with the dessert menu.
I'll be right back with your apple pie.

Serving Dishes

■ **Here ....**
Here's the Black Forest cake.
Here's your latte, sir.
Here you go.

■ **There ....**
There you go.

■ **Who had / ordered the [dish name]?**
Who had the Earl Grey tea?
Who ordered the tiramisu?

Explaining Additional Items

■ **The [item] is for the + N.**
The milk **is for the** coffee.
The chocolate syrup **is for the** vanilla ice cream.

Warning Guests

■ **Careful. The N is + Adj.**
Careful. The plate **is** really hot.
Careful. The soup **is** very spicy.

Checking In

■ **How is + N?**
How is everything?
How is the cake?

■ **Is everything + Adj.?**
Is everything OK?
Is everything good so far?

■ **Are you enjoying + N?**
Are you enjoying the pie?
Are you enjoying your dessert?

Offering Extras

■ **Would you like a / another + N?**
Would you like a refill?
Would you like another plate?

■ **More + N?**
More coffee?
More hot water for your tea?

■ **Would you like some + N + with / for + your N?**
Would you like some ice cream **with your** apple pie?
Would you like some milk and sugar **for your** tea?

Taking Leave of a Guest

■ **... anything ....**
Is there **anything** else I can get you?
Is there **anything** else you need?
Let me know if you need **anything**.

■ **Enjoy your + N!**
Enjoy your meal!
Enjoy your desserts!

 # Listening

Listen and complete these conversations.

S = Server   G = Guest

1 Getting Dishes 🎧 Mp3 73 ─────────────────────

S _____ cappuccino?

G Oh, I did.

S Great. _____. I'll be _____ your dessert.

2 Serving Dishes 🎧 Mp3 74 ─────────────────────

S _____ tiramisu?

G That's mine.

S OK, and _____ apple pie, ma'am.

3 Explanations and Warnings 🎧 Mp3 75 ─────────────────────

S The cream and sugar _____ English breakfast tea.

G Thanks.

S You're welcome, _____. The teapot _____!

4 Taking Leave of a Guest 🎧 Mp3 76 ─────────────────────

S Is there _____?

G No, I think that's it.

S OK. _____ if you need anything. _____ desserts.

5 Explaining the Wait 🎧 Mp3 77 ─────────────────────

S I'll _____, ma'am.

G Thank you. But what about my crème brûlée?

S The crème brûlée _____. I'll _____ as soon as it's ready.

134

6 Checking In 🎧 Mp3 78 ─────────────────────────

S _____? Are you all _____?

G Yes! Everything's wonderful.

S Great. Is there _____?

7 Offering Extras 🎧 Mp3 79 ─────────────────────────

S Would you like _____?

G Yes, please.

S Are you drinking _____ or _____?

G Decaf.

S _____. Is there _____?

G Maybe a few extra napkins.

S OK. I'll _____ some napkins.

Offering and Recommending Desserts

Desserts and after-dinner drinks can be very profitable for the restaurant, so servers are often asked to strongly encourage guests to spend a little more money on these items. Decide if the each of the following sentences is an offer (O) or a recommendation (R).

1. __O__ Would you care for dessert?
2. __R__ If you love chocolate, you have to try our Black Forest cake.
3. _____ Our apple pie is excellent!
4. _____ The Earl Grey tea is a good choice if you want to relax.
5. _____ If you don't try the strawberry ice cream, you'll regret it!
6. _____ Our Black Forest cake is a slice rich chocolate cake topped with hot fudge, black cherries, whipped cream, and pieces of chocolate.
7. _____ Our espresso is the best in Taipei!

8. _____ Would you like to see our dessert menu?

9. _____ The tiramisu is good, if you're in the mood for something rich.

10. _____ How about some ice cream or chocolate cake?

11. _____ The crème brûlée is quite rich, so if you prefer something lighter, I recommend the apple pie.

12. _____ The apple pie is our most popular dessert.

13. _____ Did you save any room for dessert?

 # Clearing the Table and Wrapping Up

Complete the conversations below with the sentences in the box. You can use more than one sentence for some of the conversations.

■ Try the cake next time!

■ Did you enjoy your meal?

■ May I clear the table?

■ Are you done with your pie?

■ Would you like me to wrap that up for you?

■ May I take your plate, sir?

■ Are you finished with that?

■ Would you like to take that home?

■ How was everything this evening?

---

1. Server: <u>Would you like a box for that?</u>

    Guest: No, thanks.

2. Server: _____

    Guest: No, I'm still working on it.

3. Server: _____

    Guest: That would be great, thanks.

4. Server: _____

    Guest: Not bad, thanks.

5. Server: _____

    Guest: Yes, everything was great, thanks.

6. Server: _____

    Guest: OK, I will.

7. Server: _____

    Guest: Yeah, I'm done with it.

 # Role Play

Use the vocabulary and phrases you've practiced in this chapter to act out these scenes.

Scene 1

Guest: You are very hard to please (and you always change your mind). Keep requesting things of your server.

Server: You are very busy, but one guest keeps asking you bring tableware, food, and drinks, and then asks you to take them away again. Don't loose your cool.

Scene 2

Server: Encourage your guest to have dessert.

Guest: You want to order dessert, but are afraid it will ruin your diet.

Scene 3

Server: Ask your guest about his or her dining experience.

Guest: You have many suggestions to improve the restaurant.

 # Discussion

Do you agree or disagree with the following statements? Why or why not?

1. _____ The best servers are the friendliest servers.

2. _____ The best servers are fast and efficient, but stay out of the way.

3. _____ Servers should be seen, not heard.

4. _____ Guests have the right to be picky because they're paying for their meals.

5. _____ If a guest says they don't want dessert, it's OK to recommend a dessert anyway.

6. _____ It's better to offer too little service than too much.

CHAPTER 13

The Bar

In this chapter ...

Taking Drink Orders
Describing drinks, offering specials, taking orders, receiving payment

Vocabulary
Beer, wine, mixed drinks, and cocktails

Advanced Skills
Recommending drinks, making small talk with guests

Conversation

Mp3 80

Listen to the conversation and then take turns practicing it with a partner.

B = Bartender   G = Guest

B   Hey there. What can I get you?

G   It's a pretty long list. Are you ready?

B   Sure, go ahead.

G   Well, first I'd like a beer —

B   What kind of beer would you like? We've got everything from Duvel to Taiwan Beer.

G   Hmm. I'll have a pint of Guinness, if you have it.

B   We sure do. Anything else?

G   Yes, my friend would like a glass of your house wine.

B   Red or white?

G   Which one do you recommend?

B   Well, it really depends on your friend's taste. The white is crisp and light, while the red is more complex.

G   Oh, he'll definitely want the red, then.

B   Great. One glass of the house red coming right up.

G   And a scotch, too, please.

B   How would you like the scotch? Neat, with water, or on the rocks?

G   On the rocks.

B   OK, one scotch on the rocks. Is there anything else I can get you?

G   Yeah, I think I should get something for my boyfriend. He's not a big drinker, though.

B   Well, what about a Fuzzy Navel? It's our special of the month, and half-price during happy hour.

G   What's in it?

B   Peach liqueur and orange juice. It's very popular with light drinkers.

G   That sounds perfect! He'll love it.

B   Great. So that's one Guinness, one glass of house red, one scotch on the rocks, and one Fuzzy Navel.

■ pint [paɪnt] *n.* 品脫（英美容量或液量名）

■ house wine 招牌酒

■ crisp [krɪsp] *adj.* 爽口的

■ complex [ˈkɑmplɛks] *adj.* 複雜的

■ neat [nit] *adj.* 純的

■ on the rocks 加冰塊

■ liqueur [lɪˈkɜ] *n.* 利口酒（具甜味而芬芳的烈酒）

Beer

Study the following beer-related vocabulary.

Types of Beer

Lager 精釀啤酒

Ale / Pale Ale 麥酒／淡啤酒

Pilsner 皮爾森啤酒

Porter 波特啤酒

Stout 大麥黑啤酒

Categories of Beer

Domestic 國產的

Imported 進口的

Bottled 瓶裝的

On tap 桶裝的

Microbrew 微釀的

Country of Origin

Asahi 朝日啤酒（日本）

Bass 巴斯啤酒（英國）

Beck's 貝克啤酒（德國）

Budweiser 百威啤酒（美國）

Carlsberg 卡斯柏啤酒（丹麥）

Corona 可樂那啤酒（墨西哥）

Duvel 杜瓦啤酒（比利時）

Foster's 佛斯特啤酒（澳洲）

Guinness 健力士啤酒（愛爾蘭）

Heineken 海尼根啤酒（荷蘭）

Wine

For each of the wines presented, indicate whether it's a red (R) or a white (W) wine.

R Bordeaux 波多葡萄酒

___ Sauvignon Blanc 白索維農葡萄酒

___ Burgundy 勃艮第葡萄酒

___ Riesling 雷斯林葡萄酒

___ Chardonnay 夏敦埃葡萄酒

___ Cabernet Sauvignon 卡百內葡萄酒

___ Merlot 默爾樂葡萄酒

___ Chablis 沙百里葡萄酒

Indicate the type of wine, red (R) or white (W), that pairs best with these foods.

<u>W</u> pasta with cream sauce 奶油義大利麵

_____ strong cheeses 重乳酪

_____ dark chocolate 黑巧克力

_____ fish 魚

_____ lamb 小羊肉

_____ oysters 牡蠣

_____ chicken 雞肉

_____ beef 牛肉

_____ Asian food 亞洲菜

_____ pasta with tomato sauce 番茄義大利麵

Practice making wine recommendations based on food pairings with sentences like these:

> **A** [wine] **would go well with the** [food].
>
> **I think our** [wine] **would go nicely with your** [food].

Ex. fish **A Chardonnay would go well with the fish.**

steak **I think our Cabernet Sauvignon would go nicely with your steak.**

Food			
chicken chow mein	Peking duck	prime rib	fettuccine Alfredo
lamb chops	pasta marinara	seafood omelet	grilled salmon

Mixed Drinks and Cocktails

Fill in each blank with the appropriate word from the list below.

neat	**on the rocks**	**frozen**
shaken	**straight up**	**stirred**

Isn't it amazing how many different ways there are to enjoy a drink? My boyfriend, for example, takes his whisky _____, which means he drinks it at room temperature with nothing added. My brother, on the other hand, likes his whisky _____, which means with ice. My roommate enjoys her whisky cold, but she doesn't like ice cubes in hers, so she gets her whisky _____: chilled with ice cubes and then strained. My sister, on the other hand, loves ice. She gets her margaritas _____, which means blended with ice. My best friend prefers martinis, and like James Bond, she has them "_____, not _____." As for me, I don't really care what I'm drinking as long as I'm spending time with the people I love best!

The Cocktail Menu

Look over the cocktails menu below and use it to practice taking drink orders with a partner. Refer to the patterns below, the bartender's guide on page 180, and the phrases on Page 124.

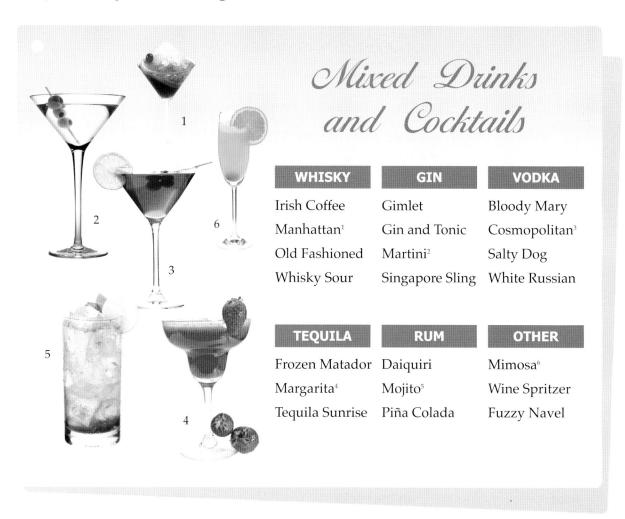

Mixed Drinks and Cocktails

WHISKY	GIN	VODKA
Irish Coffee	Gimlet	Bloody Mary
Manhattan[1]	Gin and Tonic	Cosmopolitan[3]
Old Fashioned	Martini[2]	Salty Dog
Whisky Sour	Singapore Sling	White Russian

TEQUILA	RUM	OTHER
Frozen Matador	Daiquiri	Mimosa[6]
Margarita[4]	Mojito[5]	Wine Spritzer
Tequila Sunrise	Piña Colada	Fuzzy Navel

Patterns

Guest: What's a __wine spritzer__ ?

Bartender: It's __wine__ and __soda water__ .

Guest: What's in a __whisky sour__ ?

Bartender: It has __whisky__ , __lemon juice__ , and __sugar__ .

Sentence Patterns

Study and practice these patterns.

Discussing Times with Guests

- **... from [time] to [time].**
  We're open **from** 3:00 **to** 2:00.
  Happy hour is **from** 5:00 **to** 7:00.

- **We close at / in ....**
  We close at 1:30.
  Last call, everybody. **We close in** half an hour.

Offering Specials

- **Our special [time] is the [drink name].**
  Our special tonight **is the** lychee martini.
  Our special this month **is the** mojito.

- **[Drink name] are Adj. from [time] to [time].**
  It's happy hour, so all draft beers **are** half-off **from** 4:00 **to** 7:00.
  Tequila shots **are** $100 **from** 6:00 **to** 8:00.

Asking for Orders

- **What ...?**
  What would you like to drink?
  What can I get you?
  What'll you have?
  What'll it be?

Offering Choices

- **Would you like ... or ...?**
  Would you like the house red **or** the house white?
  Would you like that from the tap **or** do you want a bottle?

Drink Specifications

- **How would you like your N?**
  How would you like your whisky?

- **Would you like that Adj. or Adj.?**
  Would you like that neat **or** on the rocks?

Keeping a Tab

- **Would you like me to V ...?**
  Would you like me to open a tab?
  Would you like me to start a tab for you?

Offering Another Drink

- **... another ...?**
  Another drink, sir?
  Would you like **another** Manhattan?

Encouraging Moderation

- **How about a [non-alcoholic drink] ...?**
  How about a Coke?
  How about a cup of coffee instead?

Asking for Payment

- **That ....**
  That comes to $2,300.
  That'll be $850.

- **Would you like me to charge that to your ...?**
  Would you like me to charge that to your card?
  Would you like me to charge that to your room?

 # Listening

Listen and complete these conversations.

B = Bartender   G = Guest

❶ Taking Beer Orders   🎧 Mp3 81

B What _____ to drink?

G I'll have an Asahi.

B Would you like that _____ or do you _____?

❷ Taking Wine Orders   🎧 Mp3 82

B What _____?

G Wine, please. We've ordered fish, so what do you recommend?

B A Riesling _____ the fish. If you want something drier, I think our Sauvignon Blanc _____ your meal.

❸ Taking Cocktail Orders   🎧 Mp3 83

B What'll _____?

G I'll have a margarita, please.

B _____ on the rocks _____ frozen?

❹ Offering Another Drink   🎧 Mp3 84

B What'll _____?

G Another of the same, please.

B OK. One Manhattan _____ .

❺ Happy Hour Specials   🎧 Mp3 85

B _____ 3:00 _____ 6:00.

G So are you offering any specials, then?

B Yes, tequila shots _____ .

6 Opening a Tab   🎧 Mp3 86

B Would you like to _____, ma'am?

G Yeah, I would. Thanks.

B Great. _____ credit card, please?

7 Encouraging Moderation   🎧 Mp3 87

G Get me another shot of whisky!

B _____ a cup of coffee _____?

G Coffee?

B Yes. It's on the house.

8 Receiving Payment   🎧 Mp3 88

B One martini, _____ margaritas, and _____ scotch _____.

G Yup, that's right.

B OK, _____ $1,250.

 # Making Recommendations

Using the decision tree below and conversation on the next page as guides, practice making mixed drink and cocktail recommendations with a partner. The bartender's guide on page 180 and the phrases on page 124 may also be useful.

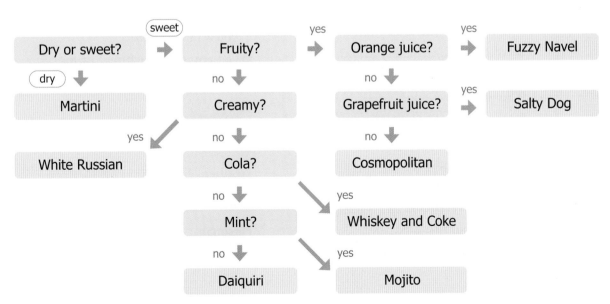

Conversation: Recommending a Cocktail

G = Guest   B = Bartender

G I'd like a cocktail, but I can't decide what to order.

B Well, would you like something dry or something sweet?

G Sweet, I guess.

B How about something fruity?

G That sounds good.

B Maybe with grapefruit juice?

G Actually, I don't care for grapefruit juice.

B How about orange juice, then?

G Yeah, I like orange juice.

B Well, what about a Fuzzy Navel?

G A Fuzzy Navel? What's in a Fuzzy Navel?

B Peach liqueur and orange juice.

G That sounds great. Thanks.

B OK, one Fuzzy Navel coming up!

 # Making Small Talk

Identify the type of small talk each of these questions belongs to.

Questions

❶ Where are you from?

❷ What brings you to Taiwan?

❸ Would you like another drink?

❹ Enjoying the weather in Taipei?

❺ So what do you do?

❻ How do you like it here?

❼ How's it going?

❽ It's a nice night, isn't it?

❾ Isn't the humidity terrible?

❿ How is everything?

⓫ Is this your first time here?

⓬ Are you used to the heat yet?

⓭ Hey, what's up?

⓮ Where do you work?

⓯ Oh, you're from New York! Are you a Yankees fan?

⓰ Get any good pictures? (if the guest is holding camera)

Category

Basic Greeting: ③

Weather:

Visit-Related:

Personal:

Role Play

Use the vocabulary and phrases you've practiced in this chapter to act out these scenes.

Scene 1

Guest: Order drinks for your table. Your mother wants a cocktail, your father wants a glass of wine, and your friend wants a beer. You just want a soda. Each person is picky about his or her drink.

Bartender: Take a guest's order. The guest has specific instructions for how each drink should be prepared. Open a tab for the guest.

Scene 2

Guest: You're drunk, but still want to have a few more drinks.

Bartender: A drunk guest keeps ordering alcoholic drinks. Try to get the guest back to his or her room safely.

Scene 3

Guest: You'd like a cocktail, but have no idea what to order.

Bartender: Help a guest decide on a cocktail. Use the decision tree and conversation in the previous section.

Discussion

Discuss the following questions.

1. When chatting with guests, what topics are inappropriate to talk about? Why?

2. What is the best way to deal with a drunk customer?

3. What is the best way to deal with a guest who is causing trouble?

4. How should you handle customers who are hitting on you?

CHAPTER 14

The Bill

In this chapter ...

■ **Receiving Payment**
Asking about the guest's meal, presenting and explaining the bill

■ **Vocabulary**
Numbers, money, and payment options

■ **Advanced Skills**
Addressing problems with bill, handling room service and takeout orders

 **Conversation**

Listen to the conversation and then take turns practicing it with a partner.

S = Server   G = Guest

S So how was everything this evening?

G Wonderful. The burger was amazing.

S It's one of my favorites too. I'm glad you enjoyed it.

G My wife's fish was a little too salty for her, though.

S Oh, I'm sorry to hear that. I'll be sure to let our chef know.

G Well, other than that, everything was great.

S Good! Are you ready for the check, then?

G Yeah, I think so.

S All right. I have it right here for you.

G Do you guys take credit cards?

S Yes, we take VISA, MasterCard, American Express, and JCB.

G OK, and is the service charge included in the bill?

S Yes, it is. Would you like me to wrap up the burger for you, by the way?

G Oh, yes, please. And the fries, too.

S Got it. OK, I'll be right back with this. And I'll take the check for you whenever you're ready. Do you need parking validation?

G Yeah, I do, actually.

S All right, just put the parking ticket together with the bill, and I'll take care of it for you. I'll be back in just a moment.

G Thank you.

▓ salty [ˈsɔltɪ] *adj.* 鹹的

▓ check [tʃɛk] *n.* 帳單

▓ service charge 服務費

▓ validation [ˌvæləˈdeʃən] *n.* 確證；確認

Payment Vocabulary

Complete the sentences with the phrases in the box.

comes to	**separate checks**	**charge it to**
ready for the bill	**pay at the register**	**your change**
accept credit cards	**wrap that up**	**service charge**

1. Would you like me to _____wrap that up_____ for you?

2. Are you _____?

3. Is this on _____ or on one bill?

4. You can _____ when you're ready.

5. That _____ $1,480.

6. A ten percent _____ is included in the bill.

7. Would you like me to _____ your room?

8. Yes we _____.

9. I'll be back in just a minute with _____.

Numbers

Study the following guide on number pronunciation. Familiarize yourself with the patterns.

1		10	ten	
		15	fifteen	
2		20	twenty	
		25	twenty-five	
3		30	thirty	
		35	thirty-five	
4		40	forty	
		45	forty-five	
5	hundred	50	fifty	
		55	fifty-five	
6		60	sixty	
		65	sixty-five	
7		70	seventy	
		75	seventy-five	
8		80	eighty	
		85	eighty-five	
9		90	ninety	
		95	ninety-five	
	1,000 = one thousand			

Read each of the following amounts out loud using the table above as a guide. Take turns with a partner.

1. $110   One hundred (and) ten dollars / A hundred (and) ten dollars

2. $215 _____

3. $320 _____

4. $1,000 _____

5. $2,025 _____

6. $8,413 _____

7. $3,500 _____

8. $845 _____

9. $350,000 _____

10. $948.50 _____

The Bill

Study the following bill and answer the questions below.

```
                    Club Café
                  09/13 13:48


   Table No.: 12        Guest(s): 2
                  Server: Lisa


                         Amount (NT)
   Qty Item
   ------------------------------------
                              250
   1 BURGER
              w/ fries
                              300
   1 LASAGNA                    80
   2 LEMONADES
                     + 10%     63
   ------------------------------------

   Total:                    693
```

1. Server's name: _____

2. Number of customers: _____

3. The meaning of "Qty": _____

4. Most expensive item: _____

5. Cost of a glass of lemonade: _____

6. Service charge: _____

7. Total: _____

8. Change out of $1,000: _____

Sentence Patterns

Study and practice these patterns.

Asking about the Meal

- **So how was everything ...?**
  So how was everything tonight?
  So how was everything this afternoon?

Asking about Wrapping Up Food

- **Would you like (me) to V?**
  Would you like to take that home?
  Would you like me to wrap that up for you?

Asking about the Bill

- **Are you ready for the N?**
  Are you ready for the bill / check?

- **Would you like this on ... or on ...?**
  Would you like this on one bill **or on** separate checks?

Discussing Payment Options

- **Would you like to pay by ... or ...?**
  Would you like to pay by cash **or** charge?
  Would you like to pay by cash, credit, **or** hotel voucher?

- **We accept N, N, and N.**
  We accept cash, credit, **and** traveler's checks.
  We accept Visa, MasterCard, **and** American Express.

- **Would you like to charge N to your room?**
  Would you like to charge this **to your room**, sir?
  Would you like to charge the bill **to your room**, Ms. Winter?

- **I'll / You can take that ... whenever you're ready.**
  I'll take that whenever you're ready.

You can take that to the cashier **whenever you're ready.**

Receiving Payment and Giving Change

- **That comes to / will be [amount].**
  That comes to $2,300, sir.
  That'll be $450, please.

- **May I V your N, please?**
  May I see **your** room key, **please**?
  May I have **your** room number, **please**?

- **... breakfast vouchers?**
  Do you have **breakfast vouchers**?
  Did you bring your **breakfast vouchers**?

- **Actually, the N is included in the N.**
  Actually, the tip **is included in the** bill.
  Actually, the service charge **is included in the** check.

- **[amount] is your change.**
  $700 **is your change**. Thank you.
  $50 **is your change**. There you go.

Seeing a Guest Off

- **Here's your ....**
  Here's your receipt.
  Here's your parking validation.

- **Thank you ....**
  Thanks you so much.
  Thanks you for coming. Take care.

 **Listening**

Listen and complete these conversations.

G = Guest   S = Server

❶ Asking about the Meal 🎧 Mp3 90

   S So, _____ tonight?

   G Good, thanks.

   S _____ wrap that up for you?

   G Sure, that would be great.

❷ Asking about the Bill 🎧 Mp3 91

   S _____ for the check?

   G Yes, I think so.

   S _____ on one bill or on separate checks?

   G All together is fine.

   S OK, _____ whenever you're ready.

❸ Discussing Payment Options 🎧 Mp3 92

   G Can I use my American Express card?

   S No, I'm sorry. _____ Visa, MasterCard, and JCB.

   G Hmm. I'm not sure I have enough cash on me.

   S Would you like to _____, sir?

❹ Receiving Cash and Giving Change 🎧 Mp3 93

   S _____ $1,480, please.

   G Here you go.

   S Thank you very much, sir. $520 _____.

   G Could I get some hundred-dollar bills for the tip.

   S Actually, the service charge _____ bill.

⑤ Receiving Vouchers 🎧 Mp3 94

> **S** Good morning. Two for breakfast?
>
> **G** Yes.
>
> **S** Did you bring _____?
>
> **G** Oh, no. I left them up in the room.
>
> **S** That's OK. _____ room number, please?

⑥ Seeing a Guest Off 🎧 Mp3 95

> **S** _____ , and _____ .
>
> **G** OK, thank you.
>
> **S** _____ for coming. Take care.

Addressing Problems with the Bill

Choose an appropriate response to each of the scenarios below, or create your own. Some have more than one possible answer.

Responses

> **A.** The tip is included in the service charge.
>
> **B.** Oh, I'm so sorry. I'll inform the cashier right away.
>
> **C.** I'm sorry about that. I'll take it off the bill.
>
> **D.** The $100 is for your two Cokes, and the $200 is for the garlic bread.
>
> **E.** May we please have some form of ID to hold on to until you get back?
>
> **F.** Could your guest stay here until you return, please?
>
> **G.** I'm so sorry for the mistake. I'll get you another check right away.
>
> **H.** The $850 is for the lobster, which wasn't listed on the menu.

Scenarios

1. _____ A guest asks if he should tip.

2. _____ A guest was charged for something she didn't order.

3. _____ A guest's bill has something that he ordered but never came.

4. _____ A guest thinks she is being overcharged, but she's actually misreading the bill.

5. _____ A guest is confused about a charge that is much higher than the other items on his bill.

6. _____ A guest left her wallet at home. She came alone.

7. _____ A guest left his wallet at home. He came with a friend.

 # Room Service and Takeout Orders

Decide if the following phrases are most likely to be used when taking room service orders, takeout orders, or both.

1. May I have your room number, please?
- ☑ Room Service
- ☐ Takeout
- ☐ Both

2. How may I help you this afternoon?
- ☐ Room Service
- ☐ Takeout
- ☐ Both

3. What would you like to order?
- ☐ Room Service
- ☐ Takeout
- ☐ Both

4. That'll be $620. Would you like to pay with cash or credit?
- ☐ Room Service
- ☐ Takeout
- ☐ Both

5. That'll be $3,110. Would you like me to charge it to your room?
- ☐ Room Service
- ☐ Takeout
- ☐ Both

6. We'll have that delivered in 30 minutes or less.
- ☐ Room Service
- ☐ Takeout
- ☐ Both

7. Thank you for your order!
- ☐ Room Service
- ☐ Takeout
- ☐ Both

8. Would you like a bag to hold everything in?
- ☐ Room Service
- ☐ Takeout
- ☐ Both

9. Please have a seat. It'll take about 20 minutes.
- ☐ Room Service
- ☐ Takeout
- ☐ Both

10. Would you like a glass of water or juice while you wait?

☐ Room Service   ☐ Takeout   ☐ Both

11. So that's one club sandwich with fries, one veggie burger with a side salad, and two iced teas.

☐ Room Service   ☐ Takeout   ☐ Both

12. Would you like us to send up some complimentary fruit with your meal?

☐ Room Service   ☐ Takeout   ☐ Both

 # Role Play

Use the vocabulary and phrases you've practiced in this chapter to act out these scenes.

Scene 1

Guest: You are a foreigner in Taiwan, and don't know how to read the bill. Ask a lot of questions about how you were charged, whether tip was included, if the restaurant takes credit cards, and so on.

Server: Explain the bill to a foreign guest.

Scene 2

Guest: Order a meal to go. As the cashier hands you your food, you realize you left your wallet at home.

Cashier: Take a guest's takeout order. When the order is ready, you discover the guest didn't bring any money.

Scene 3

Guest: You were overcharged and you are not happy about it. Point out the mistakes on your bill to your server and demand an explanation for each.

Server: A guest is angry about being overcharged, but you realize that the guest has misread the bill. Explain the charges while also attempting to calm the guest down. He or she is starting to disturb other diners.

CHAPTER 15

Special Events

In this chapter ...

■ **Organizing special events**
Explaining services, introducing
facilities, managing events

■ **Vocabulary**
Types of events, types of services

■ **Advanced Skills**
Upselling services, problem solving
during events

Conversation

Listen to the conversation and then take turns practicing it with a partner.

G = Guest   M = Manager

G Hi, I have a few questions about reserving a banquet room.

M Certainly, ma'am. What would you like to know?

G What is your maximum seating capacity? And how much do you charge per person?

M The Rose banquet room seats up to 250 guests. The Iris banquet room is more intimate, and seats about 150. And we usually charge $1,000 per person. Is this for a party?

G Well, actually. It's for my wedding reception.

M Oh, congratulations! Would you like me to tell you about some of our special services for wedding receptions?

G Sure, that would be great.

M Well, we offer on-site catering, of course — buffet and table service are both available. In fact, you're welcome to come have a tasting if you'd like.

G I think my fiancé and I would like that very much.

M Wonderful. In addition to catering, we also assist guests in arranging entertainment and hosts for their events.

G Oh, yes, we may need that.

M No problem. And we can also provide projectors and screens, for guests who want to show videos and pictures.

G Sounds great. Can I reserve a time to come and check out the Iris banquet room?

M Of course. We have an opening next Friday afternoon at 2:30. Does that work for you?

G Yes, Friday is good.

M And should I arrange a tasting for you then, too?

G Yes, please. My name is Polly Potts, P-O-T-T-S, and my number is 0910-012-345.

M Thank you very much, Ms. Potts. See you on Friday!

- banquet [bæŋkwɪt] room 宴會廳
- seating capacity 座位容量
- intimate [ˋɪntəmɪt] *adj.* 清幽的
- wedding reception 婚宴
- on-site catering 現場餐飲
- tasting *n.* 試吃
- host *n.* 主持人
- projector [prəˋdʒɛktə] *n.* 投影機

 # Types of Events

Complete these sentences.

1. Mr. and Mrs. Ma celebrated twenty-five years together by throwing _____ at the hotel for all their friends and relatives.
(A) a wedding anniversary party   (B) a wedding reception   (C) an end-of-the-year party

2. The restaurant manager spent two months organizing the guest's 50th _____.
(A) graduation party   (B) birthday party   (C) retirement party

3. The company's _____ is held in the same hotel ballroom every December.
(A) surprise party   (B) end-of-the-year party   (C) retirement party

4. The _____ was so unexpected that we thought grandma would faint from shock.
(A) surprise party   (B) farewell party   (C) retirement party

5. The couple decided to hold both their wedding and _____ at the hotel.
(A) reception   (B) farewell party   (C) graduation party

6. The employees decided to throw a _____ for their old boss to thank him for his hard work over the years.
(A) birthday party
(B) retirement party
(C) wedding anniversary party

7. To celebrate his leaving high school, Teddy's parents organized a big _____ for him at his favorite restaurant.
(A) wedding anniversary party
(B) end-of-the-year party
(C) graduation party

8. The students celebrated their teacher's move to Canada by throwing him a small _____ .
(A) retirement party
(B) graduation party
(C) farewell party

Event Services

Indicate the category the following services belong to.

Food (F)	Drink (Dr)	Entertainment (E)	Decoration (De)

1. _F_ On-site catering

2. _____ Off-site catering

3. _____ Host / hostess

4. _____ Balloons

5. _____ Open bar

6. _____ Table service

7. _____ Buffet service

8. _____ Projector and screen

9. _____ DJ

10. _____ Full bar

11. _____ Flowers, table ornaments

12. _____ Live band

On-site catering

Off-site catering

Open bar

Full bar

With a partner, practice a suggesting services to people organizing the following events. Use phrases like these:

- Would you like me to tell you about ...?
- We offer ....
- We can provide ....
- We assist guests in arranging ....

1. Jack and Kelly would like to have a small reception after their wedding ceremony. They want a romantic atmosphere.

2. Ms. Yuan is organizing her company's end-of-the-year party. She wants something laid-back and enjoyable so her employees can relax.

3. Ethan is planning his parents' wedding anniversary party. It will have lots of events, and will include dancing.

4. A group of employees wants to have a farewell party for their boss. They plan on showing lots of pictures and videos.

 # A Catering Contract

Study the following off-site catering contract, and then answer the questions below.

Caring Catering

"Caring for our clients' celebrations"

Service Agreement

Event date: *February 14, 2010*

Event time: *6:00 - 10:00 PM*

Event location: *Jasmine Gardens*

No. of guests: *65*

Service type (check one): ☑ Buffet Service ☐ Full Table Service

Extras (check all that apply): ☐ Servers ☐ Bartenders ☑ Tableware ☐ Seating

Terms and Conditions

A. Caring Catering reserves the right to cancel the contract at our discretion.

B. All deposits are nonrefundable.

C. Cancellations must be made at least 3 days (72 hours) before the event.

D. Additional servers, bartenders, and tableware rentals will be charged extra.

I, _____*Wendy Wu*_____, have read and agreed to this contract.

Date: *15th November, 2009*

---

1. What are the two dining options the contract provides?

_____

2. How many days prior to the event must cancellations be made by?

_____

3. What date was the contract signed on?

_____

4. Which "extra" does the client need?

_____

5. How many guests are expected?

_____

6. Which services are charged extra?

_____

Sentence Patterns

Study and practice these patterns.

Scheduling an Event

■ **We have an opening on [date].**
We have an opening on March 23.
We have openings on May 10 and May 18.

■ **We're fully booked in / on [time], but [time] is open.**
We're fully booked in August, **but** September **is open**.
We're fully booked on the second, **but** the third **is open**.

Introducing Facilities

■ **This (That) is the ....**
This is the small banquet room.
This is the dance floor and that is the DJ booth.

■ **Over here / there we have ....**
Over here we have the dressing room.
Over there we have an area for event hosts to greet their guests.

■ **The [person] can use the N for ....**
The hostess **can use the** stage **for** her introductions.
The bride **can use the** dressing room **for** changing her clothes.

Services Provided and Not Provided

■ **We (can) V ....**
We offer free tastings.
We can provide on-site catering, DJs, and hosts.

■ **We don't V ....**
I'm sorry, **we don't** offer off-site catering.
No, **we don't** give discounts for hotel rooms to party guests.

Seating Capacity

■ **We're able to seat [number] guests.**
We're able to seat 200 **guests**.
We're able to seat up to 70 **guests**.

Discussing Prices

■ **We charge [amount] per person.**
We charge $800 **per person**.
We usually **charge** between $600 and $900 **per person**.

■ **We charge [amount] per table.**
We charge $8,000 **per table**.
We charge $10,000 **per table**. Each table seats ten.

Discussing Policies

■ **We require a [amount] deposit.**
We require a $3,000 **deposit**.
We require a nonrefundable $5,000 **deposit**.

■ **Cancellations must be made ....**
Cancellations must be made three days prior to the event.
Cancellations must be made 24 hours before the event.

■ **The N is nonrefundable.**
I'm sorry, **the** deposit **is nonrefundable**.
No, **the** catering fee **is nonrefundable**.

 **Listening**

Listen and complete these conversations.

G = Guest   M = Manager

1 Booking an Opening 🎧 Mp3 97 ──────────────────────

> **G** Is the room available on Saturday?
>
> **M** No, unfortunately _____ this week, but _____.
>
> **G** OK. In that case, put me down for next Saturday.

2 Showing Guests the Facilities 🎧 Mp3 98 ──────────────

> **M** _____ Rose banquet room.
>
> **G** Oh, it's lovely!
>
> **M** And _____ we have the dancing area.

3 Services Provided and Not Provided 🎧 Mp3 99 ──────────

> **G** Is it possible for me to show pictures and videos at the party?
>
> **M** Certainly. _____ projectors and screens for guests to use.
>
> **G** Great. What about DJs? Can you help us find one?
>
> **M** No, sorry. I'm afraid _____ entertainment services.

4 Seating Capacity 🎧 Mp3 100 ──────────────────────

> **G** How many people does the room fit?
>
> **M** _____ 150 guests for full table service.
>
> **G** I plan on having 180. Will that be a problem?
>
> **M** Not necessarily. For our buffet service, _____ up to 200.

5 Discussing Prices 🎧 Mp3 101 ─────────────────────

> **G** How much do you charge?
>
> **M** We _____ $9,000 and $12,000 per table.
>
> **G** And how many people per table?.
>
> **M** Up to 10, so that's $900 to $1,200 per person.

6 **Discussing Policies** 🎧 Mp3 102

G What happens if we need to cancel?

M _____ seven days prior to the event.

G So if I cancel a week before the event, I'll get my deposit back.

M No, I'm sorry, _____ .

Upselling Services

Like hotel reservations agents and front-desk clerks, restaurant event planners are also expected to upsell services. Study the following phrases.

Decorations

- We have an excellent florist at the hotel. His centerpieces are very popular with guests.
- Guests really love our balloon decorations. Would you like us to prepare some for your party?

Entertainment

- Why don't you consider hiring a host as well? We work with some excellent hosts, and they really help the events run smoothly.
- A lot of our clients loved having a DJ to liven the party up. We'd be more than happy to help you hire one at a reduced cost.

The Bar

- A full bar would be an excellent choice, especially when you have so many guests with different preferences.
- We have some excellent bartenders here who can help you manage the bar.

Practice the conversations below with a partner. Use the sentence patterns presented in this chapter and in Chapter 1 on Page 15 as guides.

1. Guest: I'd like a projector screen and speakers set up.

Manager: (Upsell: DJ and host) _____

2. Guest: I think I want a bar of some kind at the party.

Manager: (Upsell: full bar and bartender) _____

3. Guest: I think the room needs a little decoration.

Manager: (Upsell: flowers and balloons) _____

 # Handing Problems at Special Events

How would you handle each of these problems? Use a phrase from the box or create one of your own.

- If you don't want to lose your deposit, perhaps we could reschedule it.
- OK. I'll have another table set up and let the kitchen know.
- We don't have anything available tonight, but I could remove a few tables.
- I'll bring some out right away.
- Take your time ma'am. I'll have the cold dishes served so the guests don't get hungry.
- I'll have someone take a look at it right away.

1. Party Host: We're running out of beer and wine.

   Manager: _____

2. Party Host: It doesn't look like many people are going to come. Could we move to a smaller room?

   Manager: _____

3. Party Host: We've going to need some time. My daughter isn't sure she wants to get married.

   Manager: _____

4. Party Host: We've decided to cancel the party because of the typhoon.

   Manager: _____

5. Party Host: Excuse me, there's something wrong with the projector.

   Manager: _____

6. Party Host: We've had more people show up than we expected—at least ten I think.

   Manager: _____

Role Play

Use the vocabulary and phrases you've practiced in this chapter to act out these scenes.

Scene 1

Guest: Your wedding is in two weeks and you're desperate to finish organizing. Tour the banquet room you want to reserve and ask a lot of questions about it. You don't have much money, but find out about the other services the hotel offers.

Manager: Show a guest around the banquet room. The guest is desperate to finalize plans for his or her wedding and has a lot of questions. Take the opportunity to upsell.

Scene 2

Guest: The end-of-the-year party you organized for your company is going badly. Problems keep occurring (broken projector, not enough seats, drunk boss, etc.) and you constantly have to ask the manager for help.

Manager: An event keeps running into difficulties. Help the event host solve each problem.

Scene 3

Guest: Call the hotel to cancel an event because of a typhoon. Your boss has asked you to have deposit refunded.

Manager: A guest calls to cancel an event. The guest asks for a refund. Explain that all deposits are nonrefundable.

CHAPTER 16

Review

09 Restaurant Reservations

11 Taking Orders

14 The Bill

12 Serving and Checking In

10 Welcoming and Seating

13 The Bar

15 Special Events

In this chapter ...

With a partner take turns playing the role of Restaurant Server and guest.

Server: Complete each task in order before moving on to the next mission. If you get stuck, quickly review the pages listed in each section.

Guest: Look at page 182 for suggestions about how to play your part. If the role play is too easy, feel free to cause some problems!

Mission 1 Restaurant Reservations

Mission 2 Welcoming and Seating

Mission 3 Taking Orders

Mission 4 Serving and Checking In

Mission 5 The Bar

Mission 6 The Bill

Mission 7 Special Events

Let's Start!

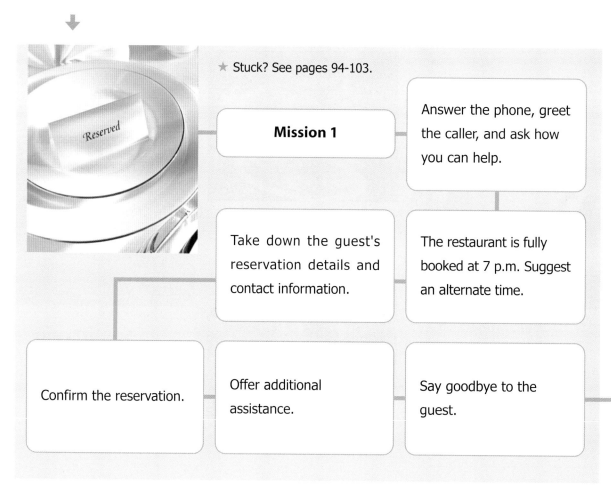

★ Stuck? See pages 94-103.

Mission 1

Answer the phone, greet the caller, and ask how you can help.

The restaurant is fully booked at 7 p.m. Suggest an alternate time.

Take down the guest's reservation details and contact information.

Confirm the reservation.

Offer additional assistance.

Say goodbye to the guest.

★ Stuck? See pages 116-127.

Greet the guest and introduce yourself.

Thank the guest for his or her order. Say you'll be back soon with the dishes.

Mission 3

Ask if the guest would like to start with a drink or an appetizer.

Repeat the order.

Recommend the fish and the steak. Explain how they're prepared.

Take the guest's order. Explain the available side dishes and ask the guest for his or her preference.

Check if the table near the kitchen is OK with the guest.

Tell the guest his or her table is ready. Lead the way to the guest's table.

Give the guest the menu. Say the server will be arriving soon.

Offer to seat the guest at another table.

Ask the guest to wait for just a moment.

Mission 2

Greet the guest. Ask if he or she has a reservation.

★ Stuck? See pages 104-115.

★ Stuck? See pages 128-137.

Mission 4

Serve the dishes. Warn the guest that the plates are hot.

After a while, ask your guests about the food. Ask if you can bring them anything else.

Bring the dessert menu and take the guest's dessert order.

Offer to clear the places and wrap up food for the guest to take home.

Serve the desserts. Ask about the guest's dining experience.

Offer to refill the guests' coffee and tea cups.

★ Stuck? See pages 138-147.

Welcome the guest and explain the happy hour rules and drink specials.

Mission 5

Recommend a drink to the guest.

Make small talk with the guest.

Take the guest's order. Double-check by repeating the order.

Ask if the guest wants to pay now or open a tab.

Ask if the guest wants another drink.

Upsell services such as entertainment, decorations, and bartending.

Say thank you and see the guest off.

Take a break!

Explain the cancellation policy to the guest. Get the guest's reservation details.

There is a scheduling conflict. Suggest an alternate time for the guest's event.

Explain the services the restaurant does and not offer.

Mission 7

Take the guest on a tour of the restaurant and introduce the facilities.

★ Stuck? See pages 158-167.

Thank the guest for coming and invite him or her to come back.

Accept payment and give the guest change.

Apologize for any mistakes found on the bill. Correct them.

Mission 6

Ask the guest if he or she is ready for the bill.

Answer the guest's questions about the bill.

Present the bill to the guest and explain the payment options.

★ Stuck? See pages 148-157.

附　錄

■ Availability Problems

A guest requests a single room, but only doubles and suites are available.

I'm very sorry sir / madam, but we only have double rooms and suites available on that day. Our double rooms are only NT$1,400 more than our singles, and come with a king-size bed, in-room safe, and large-screen television.

A guest requests a room, but the hotel is fully booked.

I'm very sorry sir / madam, but the hotel is fully booked on that day. If your schedule is flexible, we have rooms available the following day. I would also be happy to place you on our waiting list. If a room becomes available, we will contact you immediately.

■ Payment Problems

A guest wants to guarantee a room, but doesn't have a credit card with him.

Your room will be held until 3 p.m. on the day of arrival. If you'd like to guarantee your reservation, just call back with your credit card information any time before then.

A guest feels the room rate is unreasonable, and asks for a discount.

We're not able to provide a discounted rate, but I can offer you complimentary use of our executive lounge. The executive lounge has an excellent cocktail hour as well as free wireless Internet.

■ Reservation Changes

A guest wants to postpone his stay by one week and change to a smaller room.

Let me reconfirm the dates of your stay, Mr. Tang. You're arriving on September 9 and leaving on September 12, not September 2 to September 5, and will be staying in a standard single instead of a superior double.

A guest wants to cancel her reservation and make sure she isn't charged.

I have cancelled your booking, Ms. Eagen, and your credit card will not be charged. The cancellation number is JF10062408. Please keep this number for future reference.

■ Telephone Problems

You need to put a guest on hold while you speak with your supervisor.

Please hold for just a moment, Ms. Albini while I check on that for you.

(after Sorry to keep you waiting, Ms. Albini.)

You cannot understand what the guest is saying.

Please speak a little louder.

I'm sorry. Could you repeat that please?

You said you would like a suite for three nights. Is that right?

I think we have a bad connection. Could you hang up and call again?

房間狀態	表達意思	縮寫
Do Not Disturb	請勿打擾	DND
Did Not Arrive	同 No Show，有預約訂房但沒有 Check In 入住	DNA
Did Not Stay	已 Check In，但因故沒住房	DNS
Due Out	預計今日退房	DO
Sleeper	系統顯示有人住，但實際上為空房	
Sleep Outs	已 Check In，但未回旅館住宿	SO
House Count	過夜住宿的旅客人數及住房數	HC
Locker Room	員工更衣室	
Make Up Room	打掃房間	MUR
Out of Order	故障房	OOO
Occupied/Dirty	有住客但未整理之客房	O/D
Occupied/Clean	有住客已整理之客房	O/C
On Change	住客已退房，清理中之客房	OC
Occupied Ready	有住客並已整理乾淨的客房	OR
Vacant/Clean	整理完畢之空房	VC
Vacant/Dirty	退房未整理	VD
Double Occupancy	客房住兩位房客	
Over Stay	延長住宿，旅館事先不知	
Stay Over	指 Check In 時已訂好續住期間	
Under Stay	提前退房之住客	
Late Check Out	延遲退房	
Extra Bed Service, Rollaway	加活動床服務	

Hotel Reservations

Guest 1	Guest 2
Call a hotel and reserve a room.	*Call a hotel and reserve a room.*
• **Name:** Pat Lee	• **Name:**
• **Arrival Date:** May 21	• **Arrival Date:**
• **Departure Date:** May 24	• **Departure Date:**
• **No. of Rooms:** 1	• **No. of Rooms:**
• **No. of Nights:** 3	• **No. of Nights:**
• **Number of People:** 3	• **Number of People:**
• **Room:** Standard Double	• **Room:**
• **Budget:** $4,200/night	• **Budget:**

Checking In

Guest 1	Guest 2
Check in to your hotel.	*Check in to your hotel.*
• **Ask about**	• **Ask about**
- if breakfast is included	
- about restaurants in the hotel	
- what time the gym and swimming pool open	
• **Ask the location of**	• **Ask the location of**
- the business center	
- the gift shop	
- the bar	

The Hotel Room

Guest 1	Guest 2
Have a look around your hotel room.	*Have a look around your hotel room.*
• **Problems:**	• **Problems:**
- You can't find the minibar.	
- The room is hot and the windows don't open.	
- You'd like to have your suit pressed as soon as possible.	
- You need an extra set of towels.	

Hotel Services

Guest 1

Ask the concierge to help plan your day — from morning to night.

- **Interests and preferences:**
  - sightseeing
  - art
  - sports and exercise
  - shopping
  - trying local cuisine
  - the theater, classical music, jazz

Guest 2

Ask the concierge to help plan your day — from morning to night.

- **Interests and preferences:**

The Business Center

Guest 1

Turn the hotel business center into your personal office.

- **You need to:**
  - Use a computer.
  - Print out a document.
  - Have the document photocopied and mailed to a business partner.
  - Find out how much it costs to rent a meeting room and hire an interpreter.

Guest 2

Turn the hotel business center into your personal office.

- **You need to:**

The Gift Shop

Guest 1

Stop by the hotel gift shop to pick up some souvenirs.

- **You're interested in:**
  - A calligraphy set
  - T-shirts
  - Keychains
  - Postcards
  - Batteries
  - A local food or drink

Guest 2

Stop by the hotel gift shop to pick up some souvenirs.

- **You're interested in:**

Checking Out

▥ Guest 1	▥ Guest 2
Check out of the hotel.	*Check out of the hotel.*
• **Good parts of your stay:** - excellent service - delicious food	• **Good parts of your stay:**
• **Bad parts of your stay:** - the pool was very small - the view was not very interesting	• **Bad parts of your stay:**
• **Ask about these items on your bill:** - The minibar charge - The laundry charge	• **Ask about these items on your bill:**
• **Ask help with:** - Storing your luggage - Getting to the airport	• **Ask help with:**

P142   Chapter 13: Bartender's Guide (Glossary of Cocktail Recipes)

Spirits 烈酒	Fortified Wines 加度葡萄酒	Mixers and Liqueurs 調酒和利口酒	Tools of the Trade 專業用具
Whisky 威士忌	Brandy 白蘭地	Tonic Water 奎寧水	corkscrew 開瓶鑽
Scotch 蘇格蘭威士忌	Cognac 干邑白蘭地	Soda Water 蘇打水	cocktail shaker 雞尾酒調酒器
Bourbon 波本威士忌	Port 波特葡萄酒	Ginger Ale 薑汁汽水	cocktail strainer 雞尾酒濾酒器
Rye 黑麥威士忌	Sherry 雪利酒	Triple Sec 橙皮酒	jigger 量酒器
Gin 琴酒	Vermouth 苦艾酒	Grand Mariner 干邑甜酒	blender / juicer 攪拌器／果汁機
Vodka 伏特加	Madeira 馬德拉	Bitters 苦酒	cocktail glass 雞尾酒杯
Tequila 龍舌蘭		Grenadine 石榴汁	highball glass 威士忌調酒杯
Rum 蘭姆酒		Peach Liqueur 桃香利口酒	whisky glass 威士忌杯
Rice Wine / Sake 米酒／清酒		Cherry Liqueur 櫻桃利口酒	shot glass 純飲杯

WHISKEY 威士忌	GIN 琴酒	VODKA 伏特加	TEQUILA 龍舌蘭	RUM 蘭姆酒	OTHER 其他
Irish Coffee 愛爾蘭咖啡	**Gimlet** 螺絲起子	**Bloody Mary** 血腥瑪莉	**Frozen Matador** 冰凍鬥牛士	**Daiquiri** 代克里	**Mimosa** 含羞草
Irish whiskey 愛爾蘭威士忌 coffee 咖啡 cream 奶油 brown sugar 紅糖	gin 琴酒 lime juice 萊姆汁	vodka 伏特加 tomato juice 番茄汁 lemon juice 檸檬汁 Tabasco 塔巴斯哥辣醬 salt and pepper 鹽跟胡椒	tequila 龍舌蘭 pineapple juice 鳳梨汁 lime 萊姆	white rum 白蘭姆酒 lime juice 萊姆汁 grenadine 石榴汁	champagne 香檳 orange juice 柳橙汁
Manhattan 曼哈頓	**Gin and Tonic** 琴湯尼	**Cosmopolitan** 柯夢波丹	**Margarita** 瑪格麗特	**Mojito** 摩西托	**Wine Spritzer** 蘇打酒
whisky 威士忌 vermouth 苦艾酒 bitters 苦酒	gin 琴酒 tonic water 奎寧水 lime 萊姆	vodka 伏特加 triple sec 橙皮酒 cranberry juice 小紅莓汁 lime juice 萊姆汁	tequila 龍舌蘭 triple sec 橙皮酒 lime juice 萊姆汁	rum 蘭姆酒 lime juice 萊姆汁 soda water 蘇打水 mint 薄荷 sugar 糖	white wine 白葡萄酒 soda water 蘇打水
Old Fashioned 古典酒	**Martini** 馬丁尼	**Salty Dog** 鹹狗	**Tequila Sunrise** 龍舌蘭日出	**Piña Colada** 椰子波蘿雞尾酒	**Fuzzy Navel** 禁果
whisky 威士忌 bitters 苦酒 sugar 糖 orange 柳橙	gin 琴酒 vermouth 苦艾 olive 橄欖	vodka 伏特加 grapefruit juice 葡萄柚汁 salt 鹽	tequila 龍舌蘭 orange juice 柳橙汁 grenadine 石榴汁	rum 蘭姆酒 coconut milk 椰奶 pineapple juice 鳳梨汁	peach liqueur 桃香利口酒 orange juice 柳橙汁
Whisky Sour 酸威士忌	**Singapore Sling** 新加坡司令	**White Russian** 白色俄羅斯			
whisky 威士忌 lemon juice 檸檬汁 sugar 糖	gin 琴酒 cherry liqueur 櫻桃利口酒 grenadine 石榴汁 triple sec 橙皮酒 pineapple juice 鳳梨汁 lemon juice 檸檬汁 bitters 苦酒	vodka 伏特加 coffee liqueur 咖啡利口酒 cream 奶油			

Restaurant Reservations

▥ Guest 1

Call a restaurant and make a dinner reservation.

- **Number of people:** 4
- **Time:** 7 p.m. is best, but 6 p.m. is OK.
- **Name:** Quimby
- **Contact number:** 0901-234-567
- **Special requests:** table by the window, a high chair

▥ Guest 2

Call a restaurant and make a dinner reservation.

- **Number of people:**
- **Time:**
- **Name:**
- **Contact number:**
- **Special requests:**

Welcoming and Seating

▥ Guest 1

Arrive at the restaurant and be seated at your table.

- **Name:** Quimby
- **Number of people:** 4
- **Time:** 6 p.m.
- **Special requests:**
  - table away from the kitchen
  - table by the window
  - a high chair

▥ Guest 2

Arrive at the restaurant and be seated at your table.

- **Name:**
- **Number of people:**
- **Time:**
- **Special requests:**

Taking Orders

▥ Guest 1

Order a drink, appetizer, and main course. (If you're hungry, order a soup and salad, too.)

- **It's your first time at the restaurant, so ask for recommendations.**
- **Ask the server to explain anything you don't understand.**
- **You hate:** seafood
- **You love:** vegetables

▥ Guest 2

Order a drink, appetizer, and main course. (If you're hungry, order a soup and salad, too.)

- **It's your first time at the restaurant, so ask for recommendations**
- **Ask the server to explain anything you don't understand**
- **You hate:**
- **You love:**

Serving and Checking In

▥ Guest 1

Enjoy your dinner.

- **After a while, ask the server for these things:**
  - napkins
  - more water
  - a box to take food home
  - the dessert menu

- **Order dessert and coffee or tea.**

▥ Guest 2

Enjoy your dinner.

- **After a while, ask the server for these things:**

- **Order dessert and coffee or tea.**

The Bar

▥ Guest 1

After dinner, take a seat at the hotel bar.

- **Ask the server to recommend a drink. You want to drink something sweet, preferably with soda.**
- **You're with two friends — one wants a beer, the other a glass of red wine.**
- **Open a tab.**
- **You're having a great time. Order another drink!**

▥ Guest 2

After dinner, take a seat at the hotel bar.

- **Ask the server to recommend a drink. You want to drink something sweet, preferably with soda.**
- **You're with two friends — one wants a beer, the other a glass of red wine.**
- **Open a tab.**
- **You're having a great time. Order another drink!**

The Bill

▥ Guest 1

It's time to pay the bill and go home.

- **Ask if you should pay at the table or the register.**
- **Ask about the service charge.**
- **Find a mistake on the bill.**

▥ Guest 2

It's time to pay the bill and go home.

- **Ask if you should pay at the table or the register.**
- **Ask about the service charge.**
- **Find a mistake on the bill.**

Special Events	
▥ Guest 1	**▥ Guest 2**
You're planning a wedding reception.	*You're planning a wedding reception.*
· **Number of people:** 250	· **Number of people:**
· **Time:** preferably April 30, but May 2 is OK	· **Time:**
· **Name:** Quimby	· **Name:**
· **Contact information:** 0901-234-567	· **Contact information:**
· **Requests:**	· **Requests:**
- You'd prefer to have table service, but will settle for buffet service	
- You'd like a band and an MC	

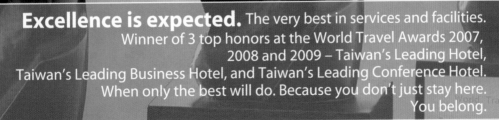

國家圖書館出版品預行編目資料

餐旅英文 = Hospitality English / David Katz, Victoria Chen 作.
－－ 初版. －－ 臺北市：
　貝塔出版：智勝文化發行, 2009.10
　　面： 公分

　　ISBN 978-957-729-763-1（平裝）

　1. 英語　2. 餐旅業　3. 會話

805.188　　　　　　　　　　　　　　　　98018347

餐旅英文 Hospitality English

作　　者 / David Katz 、 Victoria Chen
執行編輯 / 朱曉瑩

出　　版 / 波斯納出版有限公司
地　　址 / 台北市 100 館前路 26 號 6 樓
電　　話 / (02) 2314-2525
傳　　真 / (02) 2312-3535
郵　　撥 / 19493777 波斯納出版有限公司
客服專線 / (02) 2314-3535
客服信箱 / btservice@betamedia.com.tw

總 經 銷 / 時報文化出版企業股份有限公司
地　　址 / 桃園市龜山區萬壽路二段 351 號
電　　話 / (02) 2306-6842

照片提供 / 台北喜來登大飯店
　　（P10-room types, P30-hotel room, P32-minibar, P33-bathroom set, P34-
　　laundry ticket, P54-business certer, P107-pizza/sashimi/oysters, P118-seasonal
　　sautéed vegetables, P119-steak, P120-peking duck, P121-Coq au Vin, P158-
　　banquet room）

出版日期 / 2020 年 10 月初版十二刷
定　　價 / 360 元
ISBN： 978-957-729-763-1

喚醒你的英文語感！

Get a Feel for English !

喚醒你的英文語感！

Get a Feel for English !